ONLY
LIVING
WITNESS

ONLY LIVING WITNESS

Malcolm Forsythe

This first world edition published in Great Britain 2000 by
SEVERN HOUSE PUBLISHERS LTD of
9–15 High Street, Sutton, Surrey SM1 1DF.
This first world edition published in the U.S.A. 2000 by
SEVERN HOUSE PUBLISHERS INC of
595 Madison Avenue, New York, N.Y. 10022.

British Library Cataloguing in Publication Data

Forsythe, Malcolm
      Only living witness
      1.Detective and mystery stories
      I. Title
      823.9'14 [F]

      ISBN 0-7278-5520-4

Printed and bound in Great Britain by
MPG Books Ltd, Bodmin, Cornwall.

ONLY
LIVING
WITNESS

One

Peter Chapman was a small-time builder with a pretty wife, two small children and a large overdraft. Apart from worries about his overdraft his life was settled and serene. Nothing much ever happened to upset it and he was totally unprepared for the experience awaiting him at a house he was working on one glorious morning in May.

He'd begun work on the house in Great Yeldham two days before. The house stood on its own on the edge of the village on the road to Sudbury. It was a plain, box-like property built after World War II when building materials were in short supply. The day before, he had broken up the patio at the rear where a kitchen extension was to be built, and carted away the rubble. This morning he was excavating a trench for the foundations with his mechanical digger.

Peter Chapman enjoyed digging trenches. He whistled cheerfully in the cab as he operated levers and directed the movements of the shovel. There was a soothing rhythm to the repetitive movements: down ... forward ... up ... sideways ... bucket open ... then down again to repeat the cycle. At the side of the trench a neat pile of earth was growing steadily higher.

He had been working for half an hour when it happened. Just after the bucket had disgorged one of its loads there was a movement at the top of the heap of soil. Peter watched, goggle-eyed, as a human skull broke from the soil, hovered, then rolled down to the bottom and came to rest face up. He stared at it, mesmerised with shock. After a moment he switched off the engine and climbed down from the cab.

He approached the skull warily. Although there was no one in the house and the next house was some distance away, he looked around nervously before dropping on one knee to look at it. The eye sockets, filled with black earth, stared up at him like someone in dark glasses. He stood up quickly and stepped away to look down into the trench he was digging. He saw bones protruding from one side where the shovel had decapitated a skeleton.

He unclipped the mobile phone at his belt. The woman who owned the house had given him her work number. "In case of problems," she had said. Well, this was a problem all right, he told himself. He lifted the phone to ring her, then paused. And say what? *Did you know there's a body under your patio, missus?*

Remembering other cases of bodies buried under patios he changed his mind and called the police.

DCI George Millson had been at an inquiry on the other side of the county and arrived at the scene to find his sergeant, Norris Scobie, already there. When Scobie was first assigned to him Millson had asked him about his first name. "*Norris*, what sort of a name's that?" "It's Norman

French. It means 'northern'," Scobie told him. "My grandmother was French."

Millson's day had begun badly. A power failure had wrecked his morning routine, which meant breakfast without tea or toast for him and his thirteen-year-old daughter. It also meant he'd had to shave with the battery shaver he kept in the car and write a long note to their daily help telling her what to do about the fridge and the freezer if the power wasn't restored. He was not in a good mood when he arrived at Great Yeldham.

Scobie, his copper-coloured hair shining in the sunshine, was standing with the pathologist, David Duval. Duval was directing the operations of a team in gloves and overalls who were on hands and knees carefully uncovering the buried remains. Behind them a police photographer was setting up his camera.

Duval broke off as Millson joined them. "Morning, George. Good thing it hasn't been raining," he said. "It would have been a messy job if this trench had been full of water."

"What have we got so far?" Millson asked.

"Only that whoever it is didn't die naturally. The left parietal of the skull is badly fractured."

"How long do you reckon it's been in the ground?"

The pathologist shook his head. "Impossible to say until we carry out laboratory tests."

"Can't you at least tell whether or not these are ancient bones?" Millson asked irritably.

"Not without tests to estimate the rate of putrefaction. Bodies decay faster in light porous soils than in heavy. And young people with puppy fat decay faster than oldies." His eyes dropped to Millson's waist. "And so do overweight people with a high fluid and fat content."

Millson ignored the comment. "All I want to know," he said sourly, "is whether that's the skeleton of some Roman soldier or Ancient Briton you're digging up. Because if it is, Norris and I can go home and leave him to the coroner to deal with."

"Oh, the bones are not as old as *that*," Duval said cheerfully. "There's considerable staining of the ground by body fluids and I'd say the body has been in the ground less than fifty years. It's one for you, all right."

Millson grunted. "Any thoughts on age?"

Duval glanced at the plastic rule that had been laid alongside the remains. "Measures about five foot three, allowing for the skull. Could be a teenager. Equally, it could be a woman, or a small man."

"No idea whether it's male or female, then?"

"Not until I've measured the bones."

"Surely a male," Scobie said. "The rags round the legs are what's left of trousers. And those look like boots at the feet."

"Women wear trousers and young women often wear boots," Duval said tartly. "You'll have a professional opinion when I've done the post-mortem." He turned away and began speaking to the photographer.

"I think you've upset him, Norris," Millson said. "Who reported this?"

"A builder, name of Peter Chapman. He'd removed the old patio and was excavating a trench to lay foundations for an extension. The skull came up in his digger shovel. Gave him quite a shock. He's waiting in the house."

"Who's the householder?"

"Helen Forman. The builder rang her at work and she

came home. She wanted to watch, but I sent her inside."

"Right. You call up county HQ while I have a word with her. I want a specialist team up here with radar equipment and rods to probe the rest of the garden. We'd better make sure there aren't any more bodies."

The slim woman who answered his knock wore a blue nurse's uniform with white collar and cuffs. She was in her mid-thirties and her dark hair was cut in a bob. Millson identified himself and said the discovery of a skeleton under her patio must be very upsetting.

"Yes, it is," she said. "Although the body was obviously buried a very long time ago."

"How do you know that?" he asked.

"I've been watching your men uncover it through the window. There's no flesh left on the bones." Her tone was matter-of-fact. Seeing his raised eyebrows she went on, "I'm a theatre nurse. I'm used to flesh and bones." She stood aside for him to enter.

He stepped into the kitchen where a worried-looking man in workman's overalls sat at the table clasping a mug of tea. He stood up hurriedly at sight of Millson's bulk and cropped dark hair.

"This is Chief Inspector Millson," Helen Forman told him.

Peter Chapman bobbed his head. "When will I be able to start work again, Inspector?" he asked anxiously.

"I can't say at the moment," Millson said. "Not for a while, anyway."

"OK if I go, then? I've told the Sergeant what happened and given him my address."

"Let me just check something with you first," Millson said. "You're quite sure where you dug up the skull was

5

within the area previously covered by the patio? Not in front or to the side, for instance?"

"No, it was under the patio all right," the builder said firmly.

"Thank you, that's all, Mr Chapman."

The builder nodded and put down his mug. "I was relying on this job to keep me afloat this month," he said gloomily as he made for the door.

Helen Forman followed him. "I'll see they finish as quickly as possible," she promised. "I want my new kitchen put in as much as you do."

As she closed the door behind him Millson warned, "We may be here for some time, Miss Forman."

"I hope not," she said firmly. "I don't see why."

Before he could answer there was a knock on the door and Scobie entered. "The equipment's on its way," he told Millson.

"What equipment?" Helen Forman asked.

"A radar scanner and probes," he explained. "We may need to dig up more of the garden."

"Oh no! You can't. I was just beginning to make it look nice."

"They'll only disturb it if they have to and, hopefully, we won't have to do any digging. But if the scanner indicates anything suspicious beneath the ground, it will have to be dug up." He saw her open her mouth to protest and went on sharply, "This person died a violent death, Miss Forman. This is a murder case."

"Oh." She sat down suddenly. "I'm sorry, I didn't realise." She looked up at them. "Please sit down, both of you. There's an ashtray there if you smoke, Chief Inspector."

"I don't, thank you," Millson said, drawing a chair to the kitchen table and sitting down opposite her. He avoided saying, 'given up', or 'stopped'. 'Given up' implied sacrifice and 'stopped' invited questions like "When?" and "How long?", especially from other smokers.

Helen Forman smiled. "I don't either."

He returned her smile, relieved. Although he'd stopped smoking a year ago, he still suffered pangs if someone lit up in front of him. "How long have you lived here, Miss Forman?"

"About six months."

"Do you know who owned the house previously?"

"It belonged to my father. You see, he inherited the property from my aunt and uncle when they died in a car crash five years ago. It's been let since then. But at the end of last year I needed a place of my own, and Dad needed some money, so I took out a mortgage and bought it from him."

"I see. And how long did your aunt and uncle live here?"

"I've no idea, but I can tell you they couldn't have had anything to do with this body."

"Oh, and how do you know that?" Millson asked.

"Because the patio was already there when they bought the house." She picked up some papers lying on the kitchen table. "I looked these out for you. They're the estate agent's particulars when he sold it to them. They were in with the deeds when I bought it so I kept them. You can see the patio in the photograph." She handed him the papers.

He glanced at the sale particulars. The front page had photographs of the house, and in a rear view the patio was clearly visible. The other pages gave a description of the property and the dimensions of the rooms. The estate

7

agent's covering letter, dated some twenty years ago, urged Mr and Mrs Forman to make an early appointment to view.

"Thank you, this is very helpful," Millson said, passing the particulars to Scobie. "Make a note of the agents, Norris. They might still have a record of the previous owners." As Scobie wrote in his notebook, he went on, "When the press get wind of this you'll probably be pestered by reporters wanting photographs. I'll have a uniformed constable posted at the door for a while, but they're bound to get to you eventually."

"Can't you make it clear to them the body is nothing to do with me?" she asked.

"I'll do what I can, but I doubt if they'll take much notice." He turned to the door. "Thank you for your time, Miss Forman. We won't need to bother you again."

"Glad to be of help," she said with a smile.

"Nice-looking woman, when she smiles," Millson told Scobie as she closed the door behind them.

Scobie gave him a sideways glance. He'd worked with George Millson for some years now, and it was a long time since he'd last taken an interest in a woman's looks.

Millson gazed around the garden, admiring the colourful display of flowers, so different to the barren patch of ground at the rear of his own house. "I wish my garden looked like this, Norris," he said.

"I wish I *had* a garden," said Scobie, who lived in a flat over an estate agent's with his girlfriend, Kathy Benson. When he and Kathy had decided to live together there had been a choice to make between giving up his ground-floor flat in Colchester, which had a garden, and giving up hers in Tanniford, which had not. There were times when he wished they had chosen differently.

"You wouldn't have time to look after a garden," Millson told him. "Go and see that estate agent and find out who lived here before Helen Forman's aunt and uncle. I'll hang on here for the radar team."

For a while, Millson watched Duval overseeing his team pack the remains in a coffin and load it into a black van at the side of the house. After they and the scene of crime officers departed, he strolled off down the garden.

At the bottom he came across a grass-covered mound dotted with yellow flowers. A small wooden cross in the middle had BETSY written on it. When the specialist team arrived a quarter of an hour later with their radar equipment and rods, it was the first place they wanted to probe.

As they gathered around it with Millson, Helen Forman came running down the garden.

"Leave it alone! That's my dog's grave!" she said breathlessly. "That's where I buried my black Labrador."

"I'm afraid it'll have to come up," Millson said.

"NO! Don't be so heartless," she cried. "It's a dog's grave, I tell you. Oh, please leave it alone." Her eyes pleaded with him.

He saw tears forming in her eyes and turned abruptly to the men. "Leave it," he told them. "Check the rest of the garden."

"Oh, thank you," she said fervently. Pulling a handkerchief from a pocket she wiped her eyes. She turned to go, then paused. "I didn't know you were still here, Chief Inspector. Would you like a cup of tea?"

"Thank you, I would," he said. Before following her back to the house, he said quietly to the men, "You find anything suspicious – anywhere – and the dog comes up. Understand?"

They nodded.

In the kitchen Helen Forman was apologetic as she filled the electric kettle. "I'm sorry for carrying on like that – Betsy only died in January. Though it wasn't really about her. You see, she was all I had left of a relationship that went wrong." She put the kettle down on the worktop with a thump and flicked the switch. "He couldn't put up with my night duties and weekends. Bit like being married to a policeman, I suppose." She eyed him speculatively. When he made no comment she went on, "And when I saw you about to dig poor Betsy up it suddenly all came back to me."

She opened a cupboard and began taking out cups and saucers. "Where's your ginger-haired sergeant? Would he like some tea?"

"He's gone," Millson said.

"Just the two of us, then," she said. Her tone was soft and mildly flirtatious.

That evening Millson's daughter, Dena, asked him to come to a concert in the Town Hall with her at the end of the month.

"Concert? I'd be bored stiff," he said.

"No, you wouldn't. It's Verdi's *Requiem* and there's lots of trumpets and drums. You like that sort of music. Jackie's sister's in the chorus, and I promised Jackie I'd go witi her."

"You don't need me. You go."

She pouted. "I told Jackie you'd give them a lift home."

"Ah." Millson nodded. It was a lift home that was needed, not his company. "Someone else can give them a lift."

"There isn't anyone. Their dad's on tour. And they don't have a mother – they're like me."

"You do have a mother. You just don't happen to live with her. Theirs is dead," he said.

"Pff!" Dena blew through her lips. "Same thing, really."

Millson didn't approve of his daughter's attitude to her mother, but her hostility seemed implacable and he'd given up trying to reason with her. At the time of the divorce Dena had been eight and his wife, Jean, had been given custody with Millson being granted access. His unpredictable hours had made access a problem, though, especially after his ex-wife remarried and moved to another part of the country. Then, about a year ago, his daughter suddenly turned up on his doorstep one day with her suitcase, and refused to return to her mother.

"Jackie's father always seems to be on tour when he's needed," Millson complained.

"*Please*, Dad." Her voice became wheedling. "I was sure you'd come. I bought a ticket for you."

He sighed. "Oh, very well."

He settled down with half a tumbler of Glenlivet and reflected on the day. To his relief, the search team had not found anything suspicious in Helen Forman's garden. Scobie's enquiries at the estate agent's and a local solicitor's office had revealed the property had been sold to Helen Forman's aunt and uncle by a Mrs Watson. The solicitor who handled the sale told Scobie Mrs Watson had wanted a place by the sea after her husband died, and he believed she moved to Clacton. The Watsons had lived in Great Yeldham all their married lives, and he thought Mrs Watson would be well in to her eighties now. If she were still alive, that is, Millson thought gloomily. The

11

investigation was going to be difficult if all the people who had lived in the house were now dead.

He glanced at Dena, dark head bent over her homework. It had been a happy surprise when she dumped herself on him. At first, he'd had doubts about fitting her in with his job, but things had worked out well. She was more sensitive than her mother and knew when to leave him undisturbed. Silences between them were comfortable and companionable, not a source of friction as they'd always been with Jean.

His gloom lifted. Life could be a lot worse. He could still be married to her. On that cheering thought he poured himself another whisky.

Two

Two days later Millson and Scobie attended the mortuary to hear Duval's report on the skeleton that had now been reassembled on a mortuary slab.

Duval picked up the skull and held it facing them. He ran his finger over the forehead. "The size of the supra-orbital ridge at the front, and – " he reversed the skull and cradled the back of the head with his palm – "the nuchal crest at the rear, tell me it's male." He eyed Scobie. "Not whether it was wearing trousers and boots – or a dress and a bra, for that matter, Sergeant."

Before Scobie could respond Millson said gruffly, "No need to labour the point. How old is he?"

"Difficult to determine in a mature person. Up to the age of twenty-five, though, teeth develop consistently and – " he turned the skull round to face them again – "these teeth are those of a young man between sixteen and twenty. He's never been to a dentist and the teeth, together with the shape of the skull, indicate he's Caucasian."

"So, he's a young white male," Millson said, impatient with Duval's detailed explanations.

"Yes." Duval looked pained. "As for the rest of the description ..." He switched his gaze to the bones on the slab. "Medium build, height five foot four, brown hair." His eyes returned to the skull in his hands. "Now ... cause of death. Leaving aside the possibility of some other injury – a knife wound that missed the bones, for example – he was killed by a blow to the head." He tilted the skull towards them and pointed. "The fracturing of the left parietal bone indicates a single blow with a blunt implement like a hammer ... probably delivered from behind."

"How hard was he hit?" Millson asked.

"Very. The parietal has been shattered," Duval said. He put the skull back on the slab. "Next, the difficult part." With a macabre smile he laid a hand on the skeleton's shoulder blade. "How long has this lad been in the ground? The lab test on the soil samples show a clay subsoil with a high moisture content. So, being young too, putrefaction of the flesh and organs would have set in fairly rapidly and certainly been completed within about twenty years of burial. As to *when* he was buried ... well, that's more of a problem. I can only say somewhere between twenty and thirty years ago."

Millson made a face. "Can't you narrow that down a bit?"

"Afraid not."

"What about his clothing and possessions?" Scobie asked.

Duval pointed to a plastic bag on a side bench. Scobie opened it and emptied out the contents: rags of clothing, a comb, keys and a rotted pair of boots. He spread the pieces of material. "Looks like he was wearing a white shirt and denim trousers."

"So, all we have," Millson said, "is a teenager in white shirt and denims, whacked on the head with something like a hammer and buried between twenty and thirty years ago."

Duval smiled thinly. "Elliptical – but broadly correct."

"And not very promising," Scobie added.

"More like hopeless," Millson said.

At a meeting with reporters later, Millson did his best to put paid to some of the speculation in the morning tabloids. There was only one body, he told them, and it was that of a youth buried twenty to thirty years ago. He'd been killed by a blow to the head and they were treating it as murder. He appealed for information, and said he was anxious to trace a Mrs Watson and anyone else living in the house at that time.

He stressed the present occupant of the house had no connection with the crime, and had only moved there a short time ago. "So there's no point in pestering the occupier for information. And since we're making official photographs available," he added, "you have no cause to invade the garden to take photographs either, so I expect you to respect the person's privacy."

He knew they probably wouldn't, not some of them, anyway. But that was as far as he could go to protect Helen Forman from unwelcome attention.

Afterwards, he briefed the inquiry team. "There are no clues to the victim's identity," he told them, "but we know the patio was in existence when the house was sold some twenty years ago. The body was lying in a shallow grave so it was probably buried in a hurry and the patio laid on top to hide it. We need to find out who laid the patio and who was living there at the time. That means door-to-door enquiries about Mrs Watson and her family, and asking local builders if they remember building the patio." He looked round the room. "Any questions?"

"Surely someone reported his disappearance, sir. So, wouldn't he be in the National Index of Missing Persons?" a DC asked.

"There was no National Index at that time, Constable," Millson said, "and there's no point in mounting a nationwide search of every local list of twenty odd years ago until we have more information."

The initial enquiries in Great Yeldham were unpromising. There had been many comings and goings in the village in the last twenty-five years and not many of the people now living there remembered the Watsons. One or two elderly people remembered them moving in about forty years ago, and several villagers remembered a son called Tom who had left sometime before his father died. But no one knew where Mrs Watson or her son were now, and none of the local builders or handymen knew anything about the patio.

Then, a week later, following enquiries to the DSS, a WDC traced Mrs Watson to her last known address in Clacton. A visit there, and questioning of neighbours, brought the information that Vera Watson had died three years ago. She had left no will, and so far as anyone knew she had no relatives. Certainly no one knew of any son.

When she died, the local council, unable to trace a next of kin or any relatives, had buried Mrs Watson and deducted the cost of her funeral from the money in her savings account. The balance, along with the rest of her modest assets, had gone to the Treasury.

Until now, Millson had speculated that the son's failure

to come forward was due to his involvement in the murder. The WDC's information about the mother suggested another explanation: that it was his skeleton under the patio and he'd been killed by his father or mother. He decided to explore this possibility before making further efforts to locate him, and instructed the inquiry team to requestion those people in Great Yeldham who'd said they remembered the Watson family. "There must be someone who knew them well enough to tell us something about the son, and his relationship with his parents," he said.

On this second round of enquiries the team discovered an elderly lady in the village who said she had known the Watson family well. What's more, she claimed to know whose body had been buried in their garden. However, she insisted the only person she would speak to about it was the nice policeman she had seen on the local television news.

"She means you, sir," a constable informed Millson. "She's a funny old bird – wanders a bit in her mind – and she might be leading us on. We did offer to bring her in by car, but I'm afraid she won't come."

Millson grinned. "If this old lady thinks I'm nice, Constable, she deserves a personal visit."

Alice Tolley lived at the top of a hill on a council estate on the outskirts of the village. She disliked living in a council house, and she disliked having to walk up and down hill to the shops. It was bad for her legs, she told Millson and Scobie as she led them down the hall and into her back room. She longed to return to the little terrace cottage on the village green which had been her home for fifty years, and where her lifelong friend had lived next door and the shops were a few steps along the road.

"Council rehoused me 'cos they said the cottage was damp." Alice gave a snort. "It were nothing of the sort! Landlord wanted me out so he could do it up and sell it at a high old price!"

She lowered herself into an armchair and began a tirade against grasping landlords in general, and the scheming council in particular. Millson and Scobie sat down on a sofa and waited for her to finish. Instead of finishing, she went on to the subject of her family and their unkindness in never coming to see her. By now, she seemed oblivious to her surroundings and to have forgotten they were there.

Scobie's impatience mounted. He was not surprised rational people were sometimes driven to violence by the likes of Alice Tolley. Unable to contain himself he said loudly, as though she were deaf, "Mrs Tolley! Can you hear me, Mrs Tolley?"

The old lady stopped, mouth half open, and he went on quickly, "Don't you have something to tell us, Mrs Tolley?"

"What?" Alice shook her head and stared around in confusion like a drunk sobering up. "Must've bin wandering," she said. "You do that when you get to my age, you know." Her eyes lit up as they fastened on Millson. "I know you," she said. "You're the policeman I saw on telly."

Millson smiled reassuringly. "That's right, Alice. And you wanted to speak to me." He decided against a direct question about the body. "You wanted to tell me about the Watsons, I believe."

There was a delay while Alice's mind changed tracks. "That's right!" she said. "That's what I wanted to tell you. I knew Vera Watson. I lived down on the green then and she used to drop in for a cup of tea and a chat. Very nice person, she was. Not like her husband, Jim. He was a nasty piece of work."

"And they had a son, didn't they?" Millson prompted.

"Yes … Tom." Alice puckered her mouth. "He was a baddie, a real baddie. Had a terrible temper like his father. Two bull elephants the pair of 'em … always bellowing at each other. I don't think Vera cared much for either of 'em."

"Did you ever visit their house?"

"Course I did. Vera asked me back there lots of times – when they wasn't there."

"Do you remember the patio?" She gave him a blank look. "At the back of the house," he explained.

"That bit o' concrete? Is that what you call it?" She sniffed. "I calls it a yard. Yes, I remember it."

"Was it always there?"

She thought for a while. "No. It weren't there when they moved in," she said. "Must've been years later when I called one day and there it were."

Millson's hopes rose. "Do you remember when that was, Alice?"

She shook her head doubtfully and his hopes fell. "Wait a bit, though," she went on. "It were the year before Harold married Mavis."

His hopes rose again like a yo-yo. "And what year was that, Alice?"

"Can't remember," she said flatly.

Scobie, pencil poised over notebook, asked, "Who's Harold, Alice?"

"My brother, of course!" Before he could ask where to contact Harold to ask the date of his marriage, Alice's mind did a grasshopper jump and she said, "It's their silver anniversary next year."

Scobie did a calculation. "The patio was laid twenty-seven years ago," he told Millson.

Millson nodded. "Was Tom still living at home then, Alice?"

"No. Reckon he must've left about then 'cos I can't remember seeing him at all that summer."

"About how old would he be then?"

"Oh, grown up. Seventeen or eighteen, I s'pose."

"Did you see him again after that?"

"No, never. Vera told me he'd gone to Australia and was doing well. Never showed me no letters nor photos, though. She didn't seem to like talking about him much."

The possibility the skeleton was Tom Watson's, and he'd been killed by his violent father, was growing more likely by the minute in Millson's mind. "Can you remember what Tom looked like, Alice?"

The lines on her heavily lined face seemed to multiply as she concentrated. "His hair were brown ... and he were middling sort of size."

Millson's thoughts had turned to the difficulties in identifying the skeleton as Tom Watson's, and proving his dead father killed him, when Alice went on: "Come to think of it, he looked much like the other boy."

"What other boy?" Millson's tone was sharp.

"The one you've dug up, of course. Sean Kebble."

Millson glanced at Scobie who rolled his eyes up in mock despair. Millson took a breath and in a calm voice asked, "Who is Sean Kebble, Alice?"

"Tracy Kebble's boy. He disappeared 'bout the same time as Tom."

Millson frowned. "No one else in the village has mentioned this boy, Alice."

"That's 'cos everyone thought he was her brother. And she didn't think he'd come to no harm, so she didn't let on he'd gone missing. Jus' asked the Salvation Army to find him for her. They never did, though. Now we know why. Tom killed him and buried him."

"How old was Sean, Alice?"

"Same age as Tom Watson."

"Perhaps they went off together?" Scobie suggested.

Alice let out a cackle. "Not likely. Hated each other's guts, they did. Always having fights, according to Vera. Real punch-ups."

"Why did Tracy Kebble let everyone think Sean was her brother?" Millson asked, though he'd already guessed the answer.

"Usual reason," she said with a shrug. "Born wrong side o' the blanket. Disgrace it was in them days, y'see." She sniffed. "Course nowadays a girl can go off on her own and breed like a rabbit and no one cares. I dunno what the world's coming to. When I was a girl—"

Millson cut her short. "Where's Tracy Kebble now?"

"She went up North soon after Sean disappeared and no one's heard from her since. Broke her heart him going off like that without so much as a goodbye."

At a press conference the following morning Millson appealed for information about Thomas Watson. He was known to have been living in the house at Great Yeldham twenty-seven years ago, he told reporters. Also, he was anxious to trace a Sean Kebble and his mother, Tracy, who had been living in the village at that time. Tracy Kebble was believed to be living in Scotland or the north of England.

"How old are these men, Chief Inspector?" a reporter asked.

"They'd be in their mid-forties now."

"So they'd have been in their teens then. Does this mean you've identified one of them as the body?"

"No, it does not," Millson said.

"Is it possible one of them is, though?"

"It's a possibility," Millson said. "But I have no evidence of it at the moment."

Late that night, in the red light district of Leeds, a white BMW drove slowly along a street, the driver studying the girls grouped at intervals along it. At the end of the street the car turned and drove back, stopping by a girl with short blonde hair and wearing red satin hotpants. She sauntered forward. Leaning down to the open window, she began her routine patter.

The driver interrupted her. "Sandra?"

She stopped. "Yeah. We done business before?"

"No, get in."

She stood back, wary. "How come you know my name, then?"

"Never mind." He leaned across and pushed the door open.

Still suspicious, she hung back. "I only do straight stuff, y'know, nothing kinky."

"I don't want sex." He lifted a newspaper from the seat beside him and held it up. Even in the poor light of the street lamps the headlines were readable: BODY UNDER PATIO *POLICE APPEAL.* As he lowered the paper she leaned down again and looked at him closely.

"Oh, it's you? I'd never've known." She slid in beside him and shut the door. "What d'you want?"

"I want to know what happened," he said, driving on.

"I don't know anything. Straight up, I don't," she said.

"Don't mess me about. We both know whose body it is and who killed him, Sandra. So, tell me what happened."

Her voice rose. "I don't know! I wasn't *there*."

He turned the car into a deserted street between two warehouses and stopped. "You're a slag, Sandra. A good-looking one. And you need those looks to stay in business." His tone became menacing. "Now, start singing or I'll put you out of work for weeks."

"Oh God!" She turned and scrabbled at the door but he pressed the catch his side and both doors locked before she could find the handle. She became hysterical. "Don't hit me! I've never done you no harm!"

"Tell me what happened and where I can find him."

"I haven't heard from him in years. I swear to God I haven't!"

"OK. Just tell me what happened then, and I'll find him myself."

"I *can't!* 'Cos he'll know it was me told you." She began sobbing. "And he'll come after me."

"You're wasting time." He raised his fist.

Three

Thomas Watson came forward a week later. He was a middle-aged version of the youth Alice Tolley had described. His brown hair was clipped short, muscular biceps bulged the sleeves of his red T-shirt, and he glared aggressively at Millson and Scobie across the table in the interview room.

"What's this all about, then?"

Millson assessed him. A thug. His teenage traits hardened by twenty years of manhood. Alice Tolley could be right. The body was Sean Kebble's and this man had killed him.

"We believe you can help us with our inquiries into a skeleton found at Great Yeldham, Mr Watson," he said mildly. "In the garden of the house where you used to live, I believe."

"Yeah, I read about it. Don't see how I can help. I left there nearly thirty years ago."

"Perhaps you'd explain first why you didn't come forward sooner. You must have seen the appeals we made for you."

Watson ran a finger round inside the neck of his T-shirt as though it was tight. "I've bin on the road. I'm a long-distance lorry driver – Continental loads – and I've bin down in Italy the last month. I don't get to see English papers an' I don't read 'em anyway when I'm away."

Scobie opened his notebook. "Who do you work for, Mr Watson?"

"Transcontinental Haulage—" Watson broke off and pulled a card from his shirt pocket. "Here's their card. You can check it if you want." He handed it to Scobie.

Millson opened the case file. "When did you leave Great Yeldham?"

"I left home when I was eighteen and, like I said, that was nearly thirty years ago."

"What made you leave at that particular time?"

Watson stared at him. "What's that got to do with anything?"

"Just answer the question, please."

"I was fed up with the place. It's a dead and alive hole. And I was fed up with living at home too."

"Uh-huh." Millson allowed some seconds to elapse. Then, watching the man's face, he said: "Tell me about the patio."

Watson's gaze remained steady. "What about it?"

"It wasn't there when your parents bought the house, was it?"

"No. I built it for them just before I left."

"*You* built it?" Millson was taken aback by the admission.

"Yeah. They'd always wanted one, so I put it down for them as a surprise while they were away on holiday."

"You got on well with your parents, then?"

Watson eyed him suspiciously. "Well enough."

"According to our information you had terrible rows with your father."

"We had the occasional bat, yeah."

"What about your mother? When she died they couldn't find any next of kin and the local council had to bury her. Why was that? Weren't you in touch with her?"

Watson wiped a hand nervously across his mouth and shifted in his seat. After a moment he said, "Look, I don't know why you want to know all this, but I'll tell you how it was. My dad was a right bastard. He used to belt me with a length of garden hose. Mum knew how he laid into me and she did nothing about it. When he died I went back to see her. She didn't say sorry or nothing. Just said it'd never happened. That was it, far as I was concerned. I wrote her off."

Millson was thoughtful. Watson sounded convincing. But he could have fled and cut himself off from his parents because he'd murdered Sean Kebble and buried him under the patio. He leaned forward, arms on the table. "Did you know a boy called Sean Kebble?"

Watson sat back in his chair. "Yeah, I knew him."

"We've been told you hated each other and you had fights with him."

"He was a cocky little runt. Yeah, we had the odd run-in. What of it?"

"He went missing about the time you left the village, and we haven't been able to find him." Millson extracted a photograph from the file and placed it in front of Watson. "We think that could be him."

Thomas Watson stared at the photograph of the uncovered remains. His eyes widened and he looked up at

Millson with a murderous expression. "You trying to pin this on *me*? Twisting things to make out I done it? I know nothing about it. *Nothing!* D'you hear?"

Millson regarded him calmly. Watson's control was slipping. He pressed on. "What happened? One of your fights with Sean go too far? You didn't mean to kill him, but there you were with his body to get rid of. Your parents were away on holiday. So you buried it at the back of the house and put a concrete patio on top of it, then pretended you'd built it as a surprise for them."

Watson wasn't listening. He was studying the photograph intently. "This don't show the patio. What's happened to the patio?"

"The builder broke it up and removed it."

Watson's eyes flicked to Millson's face. He stabbed the picture with his forefinger. "I don't reckon that skeleton was even under the patio."

"Don't waste our time," Millson said curtly.

"I'm telling you the patio didn't extend that far from the house. Look, I should know. I laid the bloody concrete."

"Very well." Millson stood up. "We can soon settle this." He motioned to Scobie and nodded to the constable at the door. "We shan't be long."

Outside in the corridor he said, "Get hold of Helen Forman's builder, Norris. Ask him to meet us at the house. We'll take Watson out there and let him argue it out with him."

Returning to the interview room Millson told Watson, "We're going to take you to the house so you can show us exactly where you say you laid the patio. OK?"

Watson hesitated before saying, "Yeah, OK."

When they arrived at the house Helen Forman was

outside speaking to Peter Chapman. She broke off when she saw them with Tom Watson and walked quickly back inside.

The place where the skeleton had lain was now covered by a concrete base Peter Chapman had put down for the kitchen extension. Millson wished now he hadn't given permission for the building work to proceed.

"Right, Mr Watson. Show us where *you* say the patio came to."

Watson stepped onto the concrete base and up to the kitchen door. Turning round, he took two strides forward. "To here," he said, "six feet out from the kitchen door. It didn't go no further than that."

Millson turned to the builder. "Mr Chapman, you broke up the patio. Where do *you* say it reached to?"

"About four feet beyond that." He pointed. "You can see the line of it where the grass came to, and you can also see where the garden path joined it."

"That's a lie!" Watson shouted. "Listen! See that manhole there?" He pointed to a manhole cover in the path that ran alongside the house. "It was exactly level with that."

"We do have other evidence, Mr Watson," Millson said. He stepped across the concrete to the kitchen door and knocked. When Helen Forman opened it he asked, "May we please borrow that old photo you showed us of the patio, Miss Forman?"

As she nodded and turned back inside Peter Chapman moved forward. "Chief Inspector, there's something—"

"Not now, Mr Chapman. I want to deal with this first," Millson said as Helen Forman reappeared and handed him the photograph. He studied it. From a casual glance it was difficult to judge whether the patio ended six feet or ten feet from the kitchen door. What was obvious, though, was that it ended adjacent to the manhole cover Watson had pointed out. Millson felt an uncomfortable sinking feeling.

Beside him Peter Chapman said, "I was trying to tell you, Chief Inspector. I think the patio was extended at some time because about four foot of the concrete along the edge was a different texture." He jumped back as he saw the expression on Millson's face.

Some seconds passed before Millson was able to say in a calm voice, "It's a great pity you didn't tell us that before, Mr Chapman." He turned to Tom Watson. "Well, that seems to put you in the clear, Mr Watson. Is it possible your father laid this extra bit of concrete later?"

"Definitely not. When I came back to see Mum after he died it was still the same. And she'd got the house up for sale then."

"Thank you. I'm sorry we've wasted your time," Millson said. He nodded to the constables who had brought Watson to the scene in their car. "Take Mr Watson back."

"That it, then?" Watson demanded. "Just sorry? After what I've been through? Accused of murder and that."

"You heard the builder. We weren't given the right information," Millson said.

"That's not good enough. I want compensation." Watson stumped away to the waiting police car.

Millson turned towards Helen Forman standing in the kitchen doorway. "I want words with you, Miss Forman."

"Look, I had no idea the patio had been extended," she said as he and Scobie followed her inside. "This has been a dreadful shock." She led them through the house to a front room.

When they were seated Millson said, "You realise this means the body was buried during the time your aunt and uncle lived here?"

"Yes, I know." Her voice was a whisper.

"What can you tell us about them?"

She cast an anxious glance at Scobie taking out his notebook. "Very little, I'm afraid. They were called Piers and Mary, but there was a terrible feud between my father and Piers, his brother, and none of the family were allowed to meet them."

Scobie looked up from writing. "What, no one? Not ever?"

"That's right." She faced down his sceptical gaze.

"What was the feud about?" Millson asked.

"I don't know. Dad would never tell me."

"Well, we shall need to speak to the rest of the family," Millson said. "Would you give the sergeant their names and addresses, please?"

"Yes, of course." She dictated some names and addresses to Scobie. At the end she said, "I'm afraid you won't get much help from my father. He's not very well and his memory is failing."

Millson groaned inwardly. His best source of information had memory loss. "What about your mother?"

"She died some time ago. Dad's remarried and I don't think my stepmother, Christine, would know anything."

"Talk about one step forward, two steps back," Millson said, as he turned the car round and drove away. "This case gets more difficult the more we go into it. Here we have a couple – part of a family – who had a corpse in their garden. They're dead, and now we're told none of the family ever met them or knows anything about them, and the only one who would know has lost his marbles."

"People in the village must have known them," Scobie said. "They only died five years ago."

"This happened *twenty* years ago, Norris."

"Yes, but an appeal and another round of knocking on doors is bound to produce some information."

Millson nodded but said nothing for a while. Then he said, "We'll see what we can get from the family first, Norris. And I don't want reporters scurrying around stirring things up in the meantime."

Superintendent Kitchen's recriminations began three minutes after Millson arrived next morning – the time it took Millson to ascend the stairs to the superintendent's office after being summoned by phone.

"I've had a complaint from a member of the public about you," Kitchen said. "Someone called Watson. From what he says it sounds as though your investigation was thoroughly flawed from the start, and you've wasted a lot of police time. How did you come to make such a stupid mistake?"

Millson opened the folder he'd brought with him and took out a photograph. "This was taken by forensic when they arrived on the scene," he said, leaning forward and handing it to the superintendent. "You can see the cleared area where the builder had removed the patio the day before, and the trench he was digging when he stopped and called us."

Superintendent Kitchen peered at the photograph. "Where was the skeleton?"

Millson extracted another photo from the folder and passed it to him. It was a shot taken after the team had carefully excavated and scraped away the earth around the skeleton.

The superintendent compared the photos, his eyes flicking back and forth between them several times. "As far as I can see the body *was* buried in the area covered by the patio."

"Uh-huh." Millson delved in the folder and handed him a third photograph. "And that's from the estate agent's particulars when the house was put up for sale by Mrs Watson twenty years or so ago. It's taken from the back garden and shows the patio clearly."

Superintendent Kitchen glanced at it and frowned. "But this seems to confirm things. I don't understand."

Millson allowed himself a smirk. "Thank you, sir. You've missed what I missed too. If you now compare it *carefully* with the first photo you'll see the area of patio cleared by the builder goes a little beyond the patio in the estate agent's photo. Which means the patio must have been extended slightly at a later date. And *that's* where the body was buried. Not under the original patio."

Kitchen examined the photos again. "Good Lord!" He leaned back in his seat. "You weren't entirely to blame, then."

Millson thought it would have been fairer if Kitchen had left out the word 'entirely'. Kitchen was not noted for fairness, though.

Late that afternoon, in the south of the county, a man opened the door of a white BMW in the car park of the Anchor pub in Canewdon and got in beside the driver.

"All right, so you've found me," he said. "Now what?"

"I know whose body they dug up at Yeldham, I know you killed him, and I know why you killed him," the driver said.

"You know a lot, then. You must've been talking to Sandra. What are you going do about it?"

"He was my friend. You're gonna pay for what you did to him." The man in the driver's seat reached into his pocket. His hand came out holding a long-bladed sheath-knife. "And don't try to mess me around," he said.

Four

At eight o'clock that evening Millson sat next to his daughter awaiting the start of the concert in Colchester Town Hall. She had bought the cheapest seats at the rear of the hall, which were in rows of canvas chairs borrowed from a nearby school. Chairs adequate for schoolchildren did not provide an evening's support for a man of Millson's bulk, and he was uncomfortable. Also, his shirt collar bit into his neck and the bow-tie he'd been coaxed into wearing was too tight.

When they took their seats he'd been careful to interpose Dena between himself and her friend, Jackie. Her over-familiarity, and a habit of calling him 'George', irritated him. Jacqueline Delayney was two years older than his daughter. She had pale blonde hair cut short like a boy's, and a knowing look in her eyes that hinted at experience beyond her years. Millson worried about her influence on Dena. Her father was an actor who was frequently away on location, and her mother had died some time ago – in tragic circumstances, if Jackie was to be believed.

The orchestra finished tuning up and there was a stirring in the hall followed by a ripple of applause as the chorus –

a row of men and two rows of young women – filed onto the stage behind the orchestra. Dena nudged his arm and pointed out Jackie's eighteen-year-old sister. Pauline Delayney had similar coloured hair to her sister, but was otherwise quite different. Her face was innocent and relaxed, and she was plump – unlike Jackie, whose intensity and thinness made Millson suspect she suffered from anorexia.

The applause increased as the soloists came on: a slim soprano, a bony contralto, a smiling tenor and a short, well-rounded bass. They were from the local operatic society and were greeted with enthusiastic applause which swelled even louder as the conductor followed them on to the platform.

The performance began and Millson dutifully focused his attention on the chorus. Under the harsh lighting their faces were white and their mouths rows of dark holes opening and closing. He was fascinated by the different shapes and sizes of the mouths: round ones … oval … square … wide open … half closed … some showing teeth, some not. Watching the rows of regularly opening and closing apertures had a hypnotic effect, and after a while he lost touch with his surroundings and his thoughts drifted.

He found himself thinking of Helen Forman and the way her dark hair swirled when she tossed her head then returned neatly to shape. She'd produced those estate agent's photos pretty smartly on that first visit. Had she deliberately misled them from the beginning? And he was sceptical of her claim that the family knew nothing about her aunt and uncle. Families weren't like that. There was nearly always someone who knew the scandals and secrets. Had the aunt and uncle had a son? Was that whose body it was?

Millson's reverie was suddenly shattered by an ear-splitting crash of drums followed by shrieking alto voices as orchestra and chorus plunged into the double fortes and rising crescendos of *Dies Irae*. When it ended, an outbreak of applause signalled the interval.

"I enjoyed that," he told his daughter.

"Good. I knew you would," she said.

In the bar, he led the two girls to the soft drinks at the end of the counter. "What'll you have? Orange? Lemonade?"

"I'll have a lager and lime, please, George," Jacqueline Delayney said.

He hid his annoyance and spoke lightly. "You're under age, Jackie. Are you trying to get me into trouble?"

"My father doesn't mind me drinking lager," she said in an aggrieved tone.

"I'm not your father, I'm a policeman and I *do* mind," he said.

Her eyes briefly flashed defiance and then her mouth turned down in a sulk. "All right, I'll have a Coke, then."

When he returned with the drinks her face had relaxed and she said in a friendly tone, "You know this case you're on – the body at Great Yeldham?"

"Jackie, I don't—"

"Oh, I know you won't talk about work. Dena's told me. I was only going to tell you my granddad has a weekend cottage there. We stay there sometimes when Father's resting."

"Resting?" Was Delayney in ill health?

Jackie grinned. "That's what actors call it when they're not working," she said. "He gets plenty of work these days, though."

"And where is he working at present?"

"He's in Cyprus. They're making a film in the Trudos mountains. Will your men question him when they get back? He spent holidays in Yeldham when he was a boy and Granddad says they're questioning everyone who ever lived there."

Millson smiled. "I don't think they'll need to trouble your father, Jackie."

"Oh, he wouldn't mind. He likes meeting policemen. He often has to play one, you see, and it helps him get into the part."

Later that night, on a desolate stretch of the Essex coast between the Blackwater and the Crouch, a man hiding in the bushes on the sea wall lifted his night glasses. He focused them on the couple in a car parked on the farm track below him. The track ended at the foot of the sea wall – a twenty-foot-high earthwork that protected Tillingham Marshes from the sea. On the other side of the wall the tide had begun to creep in over Dengie Flats.

It wasn't the first time Jack Belcher had spied on the couple. They parked here regularly on Wednesday nights after meeting up for a drink in the Cap and Feathers in Tillingham. He reckoned they were townies from Maldon and likely as not one or other of them was married, if not both.

The first time he saw them fondling in a corner of the bar he followed them when they left and saw them drive off down a lane that led to a dead end. Mounting his bike, he followed the car's lights along the lane and then down a farm track to where the car was parked beside the sea wall. Tonight, he was in position before they arrived.

Out at sea, where darkness obscured the horizon, a dark red glow appeared like the reflection of a distant fire. The glow brightened and widened, sending red streaks across the sea and turning orange as the rim of a full moon breached the blackness and revealed the line of the horizon. It rose swiftly, faster than a rising sun, bathing sea and shore in bright moonlight.

Oblivious to the dramatic beauty unfolding over the sea, the man and woman in the car began undressing. Jack Belcher adjusted his position to obtain a better view. The night was warm and windless and the driver's window was down. He could hear every sound they made, even the rustle of their clothing as they struggled out of it in the confined space.

Behind him, on the vastness of Dengie Flats, two men were moving across the treacherous mud, their figures silhouetted by the rising moon. The leading man was floundering, sinking ankle-deep and at times up to his knees in the soft mud.

The other man wore platens. 'Splatchers', the locals called them, wooden boards strapped to his boots that enabled him to slither across the mud without sinking, in the way snow-shoes slide over snow. He was gaining steadily on the first man.

Below Jack Belcher the car rocked gently as the couple began their weekly love-making. Watching avidly, he pressed his face into the binoculars, flattening the rubber eyepieces.

On the mudflats, the pursuer caught up with his quarry at Marshhouse Outfall, where the man was sunk to his thighs in the quagmire. The exhausted captive stared up at him with frightened eyes.

"For God's sake help me! I'm stuck!" he gasped.

The other man's teeth flashed in a mirthless smile and he shook his head. "Saves me having to kill you, you piece of shit."

As the man shouted and swore, and tried to grab at him, he stepped back and said viciously, "Tide'll be in soon and you'll drown. That's if the mud doesn't drag you under first."

He turned and trudged away. Behind him, the man's frantic screams were mere whispers in the air on the vast wasteland of Dengie.

The couple in the car reached a climax and collapsed, happily spent. When they lit cigarettes and lay back, languidly smoking, Jack Belcher crawled away along the wall to where his bike was lying. Standing up, he glanced across the wet mud. It shone like a huge mirror in the moonlight. Beyond it, out on the water, something caught his attention. Raising the binoculars, he peered through them for a time. Then, picking up the bike, he trundled it down the slope of the sea wall and rode leisurely away.

The tide came in fast across the flat mud. Its deceptive gentle undulations – forward and backward, then forward again further – masked the speed of its approach. It snaked into gullies and swatchways, swiftly filling them and leaving smooth water behind as it moved relentlessly on.

Soon it reached the man trapped in the sludge of Marshhouse Outfall. His desperate struggling had merely helped the grasping mud to suck him ever deeper and it had now swallowed him to his armpits. The first kiss of the approaching water on his neck unhinged him. Flinging back his head, he began shrieking uncontrollably.

Behind the sea wall, the man in the car opened the door

to make it easier to pull on his trousers. The distant screaming sounded like the cries of a seagull, and if he had not been a town-dweller he might have known that seagulls were not nocturnal. He turned his head to listen longer but the woman's hand reached out and took hold of him again.

"C'm here," she said, drawing him back in.

In Marshhouse Outfall the helpless man frantically strained his head higher, making loud spluttering noises as the water reached his chin and undulated gently over mouth and nose.

Soon the only sound was the murmur of the tide moving on.

Five

The following morning, Scobie phoned the number Helen Forman had given for her father. A man's voice answered. "I'm his son-in-law, Quentin Page. What's it about?"

Scobie identified himself and said they would like to ask his father-in-law about the house he had once owned in Great Yeldham.

"Not much use asking him anything. Didn't Helen tell you the old man's gaga?"

"She said he had trouble with his memory and he's forgetful."

"Forgetful? That's only the half of it. He's out of his mind. He ought to be in a home."

"We still need to speak to him," Scobie said firmly.

"Oh, very well. You'd better come along, then."

Edward Forman's house in Coggeshall was a large double-fronted building of the early Victorian period. The bricks had become greyish in colour over the years, giving it a forbidding appearance. There were urns on pedestals either

43

side of the flight of steps leading up to the double front doors and to the side of the house there was a double garage with a tarmac parking area in front of it.

One half of the double doors was opened to them by a woman with wavy blonde hair. She was dressed in a navy-blue skirt and white blouse. While Millson and Scobie were identifying themselves, a man in spectacles with a toothbrush-sized moustache on his upper lip came swiftly down the hall. He was wearing grey trousers and an open-necked white shirt.

"It's all right, Christine. *I'm* dealing with this," the man said, attempting to edge her aside.

"No, you're not," the woman said, keeping hold of the door. "Are you the police?" she asked, addressing Millson.

"Yes, and who might you be, madam?" he asked.

"I'm Christine Forman, Mr Forman's wife."

Millson was surprised to find Helen Forman's stepmother was not much older than she was.

"Second wife," said the man with spectacles.

"It's not a crime to be a second wife, Quentin," Christine Forman said sharply. "Helen told me the police would be calling to see Eddie, so don't interfere."

"I was trying to save you trouble," he said angrily, stepping back and retreating down the hall.

She turned and watched him, waiting until he entered a room at the end and closed the door before she invited them in. "Quentin lost his job and had to sell his house. He resents him and his wife having to live here on Eddie's charity," she said as they stepped into the hall. "He blames me for Eddie letting Helen have the Yeldham house. His wife, Ruth, is the eldest of Eddie's children and Quentin thinks she should have had it."

"Will Ruth be in now?" Millson asked. "We need to speak to her too."

"No, she'll be at work. She's usually home about seven." She turned to the stairs. "Eddie's upstairs, Chief Inspector."

"Perhaps we could have a few words with you first, Mrs Forman," he said.

"Yes, of course. In here." She opened the door to a small room leading off the hall.

"I gather from Helen her father has problems with his memory," Millson said, as they seated themselves. "How long has he been like this?"

"I'm afraid it's worse than that, Mr Millson. Helen doesn't like to say so, but he's been diagnosed as suffering from Alzheimer's disease. It started about four years ago, soon after his brother and sister-in-law were killed in that dreadful crash on the M11. I thought he was just becoming forgetful, like we all do at times. After all, he is seventy. But it became so bad, and so quickly, he was sent to a specialist. And that was the diagnosis. It's sad to see him like he is. He's been so fit and full of life, right from the when we were married."

"How long have you been married?" Millson asked, hoping it was a long time and she could throw light on the feud Helen had mentioned.

"Eighteen years. Two years after his first wife died." She brushed her hair from her face and gave a nervous laugh. "Everyone thought it was scandalous marrying a man twice my age. You see, Eddie was fifty-two and I was twenty-six, only three years older than his daughter, Ruth. But his children were grown up and I don't think they minded much, not Helen anyway."

"Do you know anything about this feud between him and his brother?"

"No, I don't. I didn't even know they existed until they were killed in that car crash. It upset Eddie a lot when he found they'd left him everything."

"And since then?"

"Not a word."

"Weren't you curious?"

"Naturally. But when I asked him he told me it was none of my business. And he was right, of course."

"Well, thank you, Mrs Forman. Perhaps we could see your husband now."

Ascending the curved stairway she said, "Some days he's worse than others and I'm afraid you've caught him on one of his bad days."

Scobie asked, "Does he realise a body has been found in their garden?"

"I'm not sure. He has his own telly but it's difficult to know how much he takes in. Certainly he hasn't said anything. And we haven't said anything to him about it, of course."

They reached the landing. As she paused at a door, she said, "His son, Bobby, looked in to see him, but he was just leaving. So, I'll stay while you ask your questions. Strangers confuse Eddie. He thinks he ought to remember them, you see."

"We'll do our best not to distress him," Millson said. "But we do have to ask him about his brother and sister-in-law."

She nodded and opened the door. The room reminded Millson of a bed-sit he'd lived in with his ex-wife when they were first married. There was a double bed, table and chairs, and a kitchen unit with a fridge beneath it. Edward Forman and his son were sitting in armchairs either side of a coffee table. The old man wore a dressing-gown. He was white-haired and he looked frail. The son was about thirty and had dark curly hair and a boyish face. He rose to his feet.

"These gentlemen are police officers, Bobby," Christine Forman told him. "They've come to ask your father some questions."

Robert Forman nodded. "I'll be off, then." He bent and patted his father's shoulder. "Bye for now, Dad."

Edward Forman stared after him vacantly as he left the room. His wife moved forward and spoke in the tone of a parent addressing a child. "Eddie, these gentlemen want to ask you about the house at Great Yeldham. You know … where Helen lives now."

"Of course I know where Helen lives!" Edward Forman's eyes were bright, his voice aggressive. He craned his head forward and peered at Millson. "Who are you?"

Millson dispensed with formality. "I'm George," he said.

"And him?" Eddie Forman pointed a bony finger at Scobie.

"He's called Norris," Millson said.

"What d'you want?" Edward Forman's head swivelled sideways. "What do they want, Chrissy?"

"They'd like to know about the time your brother and sister-in-law lived there. Piers and Mary. D'you remember Piers and Mary?"

"Who?"

"Piers and Mary – your brother and his wife."

Edward Forman showed the whites of his eyes like an animal in fright as his brain searched broken pathways in a fragmented memory. After a moment his face slackened and his eyes became normal.

"They're dead!" he announced triumphantly. "I went to their funeral." He nodded vigorously. "That's right. Piers and Mary. Dead, the pair of them." The eyes dimmed as though the intelligence behind them had been switched off.

Millson asked gently, "Did Piers and Mary have any children, Eddie?"

Eddie Forman's eyes came alive and he gave a barking laugh. "Piers couldn't make babies." His mouth was working. "God's punishment, that was."

Millson looked at Christine Forman. She shrugged her shoulders.

Millson asked patiently, "God's punishment for what, Eddie?"

The eyes turned upwards in their sockets, searching a distant past. "Borrowed other people's ... you know ... fostering ..." His voice dropped to a mutter.

"*Are you saying they had foster children, Eddie? Boys?*"

The sudden sharpness of Millson's voice and his urgent tone startled the old man. He became agitated, rocking backwards and forwards in his chair. "Mary and Piers are dead!" he shouted. "Car crash." He smacked a fist into the palm of the other hand and cried, "*Boom!* Both of them." His gaze turned, unseeing, on Millson. "I went to their funeral."

"Yes, you said."

"Piers couldn't make babies."

Millson looked at Scobie and raised his eyes in despair. Scobie leaned forward. "Do you have photographs of them, Mr Forman? And the children perhaps?"

"Children? What children?" Eddie Forman's gaze

shifted, fastened on him. "Who are you? Do I know you?" His eyes moved back to Millson, back again to Scobie, then roved the room and alighted on his wife. Recognition flared. "Who are these people, Chrissy?" His voice was frightened. "I don't remember them. I don't know what they want. Tell them to go away!"

She moved quickly to him and put her arm round his shoulders. "It's all right, dear," she said soothingly. "Just people to see me. They're going now." She bent and kissed his cheek, then turned to Millson and Scobie. "I'm afraid you'll have to leave."

She followed them out to the landing and closed the door behind her. "I'm sorry. He gets like this sometimes. I'm afraid you won't get any more sense out of him."

"What happened to their possessions?" Millson asked. "They must have had letters, photos, the usual things."

"Eddie burnt them all ... absolutely everything." As Millson's eyebrows lifted she went on, "Yes, I know. I was shocked too when he told me. This was five years ago, after they died. Eddie was fit and well then. You wouldn't have recognised him from the poor old soul he is now. He told me he cleared all the drawers and cupboards and made a bonfire of everything in the garden. Clothes, bedclothes, curtains, carpets ... every single thing. After that he had a house clearance firm take away the furniture and everything else. Then he had the whole house redecorated and refurnished and told an agent to rent it out. It would still be rented now except Helen needed somewhere to live when she broke up with her partner, and Eddie let her buy it from him."

"Do you know *why* he destroyed all their belongings?"

She shook her head. "I suppose he wanted to wipe out

every trace of them, but I've no idea why. As I told you, if I asked questions he just said it was nothing to do with me." She sighed. "He's probably forgotten the reason himself now."

"Has he ever mentioned foster children before?"

"No, never."

"So, do you think he knows what he's saying? Should we take it seriously?"

"I think it could be true. He doesn't usually make things up, he simply gets them wrong."

They descended the stairs. In the hall, as they said goodbye, Millson said, "I'd be grateful if you'd have a good look round the house, Mrs Forman, and see if you can find any old letters, photos – anything that might help us."

"Yes, of course, but I doubt if I will. Eddie was very thorough with the Yeldham house, so I don't imagine he left anything lying around here."

Descending the front steps Millson said, "Unless the foster children are figments of old Eddie's imagination, Norris, the Social Services should have records."

"You think it's the body of one of the children?" Scobie asked.

"Well, it's an obvious possibility, isn't it? Anyway, it's a lead we have to follow so you'd better get on to the county Social Services department."

"That would mean Helen Forman's uncle and aunt were murderers."

"Not 'would mean', Norris, '*could* mean'. What's more to the point is that Eddie must have visited his brother and sister-in-law at some time. How else would he have known they had foster children?"

*   *   *

Behind them Christine Forman closed the front door. As she turned to the stairs, a door in the hall opened. She smiled as Robert Forman emerged.

"I thought you might wait," she said.

"Did the police get any sense out of Dad?"

"Only that your aunt and uncle may have had foster children. I've never heard him say that before. Did you have a nice chat with him?"

"Not really." Robert Forman sighed. "Some days he's not like my father at all – he's a total stranger. I don't know how you put up with him."

"I put up with him because I was once in love with him and he's your father, Bobby."

"It's not fair! You shouldn't have to do this."

She put out her arms and drew him to her. "Dearest and most favourite stepson," she murmured.

"I'm your *only* stepson." His mouth pouted.

She laughed lightly. "I know. You're my only anything," she said. "You're all I have. That's why you're so precious." She bent her head and kissed him full on the mouth. As he clutched at her, prolonging the embrace, she gently pushed him away.

He said hoarsely, "I wish he'd die in his sleep."

She laid a finger across his lips. "You mustn't wish things like that, darling. Wishes sometimes come true … and not always the way you meant them to."

Along the corridor a half-open door quietly closed.

Scobie's phone call to the county Social Services department was met with a discouraging response. The department had been purged, reorganised, and restaffed following recent scandals in two of its children's homes.

Searching through their records of children fostered twenty years ago would be a major task, they informed him. Especially as he was unable to supply any names other than those of the possible foster parents.

"And don't tell me," Millson said sourly, when Scobie recounted the problems, "they haven't the resources to do it."

"No, but they did say they were short-staffed and it would take time," Scobie admitted.

"Well, I'm not going public on the Formans until we get confirmation one way or the other on the foster children," Millson said. "Else I'll have Kitch blowing his top again. We'd better interview the son next."

When Christine Forman helped her husband to his bed that night he was submissive as usual. But as she kissed his forehead and turned to leave, he grabbed her hand and mumbled an entreaty. This were the occasions she dreaded. When this whimpering old man – once so virile and dominant – now pleaded with her.

Forcing a smile, she rolled back the bedclothes and knelt beside the bed.

Six

The body on Dengie Flats was discovered next morning by a warden from the nature reserve at St Peter's-on-the-Wall as he was walking along the sea wall to the decoy pond on Tillingham Marshes. A hump in the normally smooth mud caught his eye. He stopped and studied it through binoculars. Encased deep in the mud, the body had remained upright, undisturbed by the outgoing tide, with only the head and shoulders showing.

The warden hurried to the telephone kiosk by Howe Farm. As the body was on the foreshore below the high-water mark, he called the coastguard. They arrived half an hour later in a navy-blue Land Rover with a trailer attached. The warden clambered into the Land Rover and directed the driver to where earth ramps had been built either side of the sea wall to enable a vehicle to drive up over it and onto the foreshore.

After a survey of the terrain, two of the party pulled on waders and strapped platens to their feet. A wooden sled was lifted from the trailer and loaded with shovels and long planks. The two men set off across the mud to the body, towing the sled behind them. A rope attached to the rear of the sled unwound from a reel on the front of the Land Rover.

The men reached the body and laid the planks around it to form a makeshift platform. They excavated some of the mud on one side with their shovels and then unfastened the rope from the sled and looped it under the dead man's shoulders. At a signal from them the driver started the Land Rover's engine and winched the rope taut. Putting the vehicle in reverse, he gradually increased the tension on the rope.

Slowly, like a cork from a bottle, the body was drawn from the mire until, with a sudden *plop*, the suction was broken and the body hauled free. It was loaded onto the sled along with the planks and shovels. The rope was unfastened from it and reattached to the sled. Then with the men guiding it, the sled was winched in across the mud by the Land Rover.

A police car and police doctor arrived on the scene, alerted by the coastguard control. "The poor devil was stuck fast," a coastguard told one of the policemen. "He must have watched the tide coming in, knowing it was going to drown him."

"He must be a stranger to these parts," said the policeman. "The locals know better than to set foot on the Flats without platens. Even then you have to know your way round the soft bits."

The doctor laid a plastic sheet on the ground to protect his clothes, and knelt beside the body. "Nice fresh one, not long been in the water by the look of it," he remarked cheerfully.

He made a short examination and rose to his feet. "Died

within the last forty-eight hours, I'd say," he told the police officers. "There are no obvious injuries, though it's difficult to be sure through all the muck, so I'd say he probably drowned. You can send him off to the mortuary now."

On their return to Maldon police station the policemen recorded the event in the Daily Occurrence Book and notified the coroner's office.

Robert Forman's house in Manningtree was on a recently built estate of 'executive-style town houses', as local estate agents termed them. A grey Mercedes stood in the drive.

Robert Forman greeted them nervously. "I told the sergeant I don't know anything when he phoned. So why have you come to see me?"

"We're speaking to all the family, Mr Forman," Millson said. "Perhaps we could come in?" he added as Robert Forman showed no sign of inviting them.

"Yes, OK." He led them to a room at the back of the house which had been set up as an office. On the walls, above the filing cabinets and desk, there were pictures of yachts and motor cruisers.

Scobie stepped forward and peered at them. "Are these to do with your line of business, Mr Forman?"

"Uh-huh. I run a yacht chartering business – hiring out yachts and motor cruisers for holidays on the East Coast rivers and waters. The yard is at Kirby Creek on the Walton Backwaters."

He sat down at the desk and motioned them to chairs. Then, changing his mind, he brought his own chair round to the front of the desk. "My wife's not here, I'm afraid – she works in the City. But can I get you something? Coffee? Tea?" He spoke in a rush as though anxious to get the words out before he lost his train of thought.

"Thank you, no," Millson said. "We're trying to build up a picture of your late uncle and aunt, Piers and Mary, and we're not doing very well. Your sister says she knows nothing about them and your father, unhappily, couldn't help much either. Except he seemed to think they had foster children." Millson stared him in the eye. "Do you know anything about that, Mr Forman?"

"Me? No, of course not! *None* of us do."

Millson noted the vehemence. Robert Forman was intent on distancing his family from the aunt and uncle because he believed they'd committed murder. Millson was equally intent on prising out information and he'd arranged with Scobie to fire questions alternately to unsettle Forman.

Millson gave a slight nod. Scobie leaned forward. "How old are you, Mr Forman?" he asked.

Forman's head turned to him in surprise. "Thirty-five. Why?"

Millson said, "And in thirty-five years you've learned nothing at all about this aunt and uncle?"

Forman's eyes returned to Millson. "That's right." They swivelled back to Scobie as Scobie said, "I find that very hard to believe, Mr Forman."

"I don't see why. Helen's told you Dad wouldn't let us meet them, and never spoke about them."

"What about your mother?" Millson snapped, and saw Robert Forman flinch.

"You leave my mother out of it," he said angrily. "She's been dead twenty years."

"So, you were fifteen when she died," Scobie said.

Forman's head moved again. "Yes. She died a very unpleasant death from cancer which I don't want to be

56

reminded of. So stop asking about her." He sounded upset.

"Did she tell you about Piers and Mary?" Millson asked.

"*No!* Stop asking about her."

Millson noticed moisture forming in the corners of his eyes and went on, relentlessly, "Did she tell you they had children?"

"No! Shut up, damn you!" Forman shouted.

"Why are you so upset?"

"Because—" He caught his breath and turned his head away. Fumbling in his pocket he pulled out a handkerchief and wiped his eyes. "You and your damned questions!" he said angrily.

He recovered after a moment and went on, "I'm upset because your questions brought back an unpleasant incident in my childhood. It has nothing to do with your inquiry."

"There has to be *some* connection," Millson said.

Robert Forman stared at him in disbelief. "You don't give up, do you?" He gave a sigh. "All right. But it won't help you at all. It happened soon after my mother died. That's why I was upset."

Bobby Forman was fifteen. Overcome with grief, and feeling lonely and abandoned, he decided to find the uncle and aunt called Piers and Mary he'd overheard his mother and father talk about. There was a P. Forman in the local telephone directory with an address in Great Yeldham. Not knowing if this was Piers Forman, and too shy to telephone him, he set off on his bicycle to see where he lived. He found the house and hung around for a while. Then, plucking up his courage, he rang the bell.

A man opened the door, and there was a young girl hovering behind him.

"It was like suddenly coming face-to-face with Dad," Robert Forman said. "It completely threw me and I panicked. I made some excuse about a wrong address, and just fled. When I got back I told Dad. It was stupid of me, but I thought he'd be pleased." He swallowed. "Mum had just died and I think he was half out of his mind. He went berserk. He grabbed me ... picked up the dog whip ... and thrashed me with it. Then he told me never to go near them again." He let out his breath.

"That was a terrible experience for you," Millson said sympathetically.

"It was. And much good it has done you hearing about it," Forman said bitterly.

"Would you tell me about the girl, please."

Forman shrugged. "She was about the same age as me. Blonde bubble curls ... big blue eyes ... I remember thinking she was pretty."

Millson nodded and stood up. "Thank you for telling us this, Mr Forman, and I'm sorry to have upset you. But—"

"Fat lot you care!" Forman said angrily.

"That was hard work for very little," Millson said as he got into the car and began pulling on his seat belt.

"It was diabolical work. It was out of order, the way you treated him, *sir*."

Millson head jerked round. When Scobie joined him three years ago on transfer from the Metropolitan Police he'd been accustomed to calling his boss 'guv'nor'.

"Don't ever call me guv'nor!" Millson had bellowed at him on their first day together. "Schools and prisons have governors. I'm an inspector."

"Yes, *sir*," Scobie had said smartly.

"And you can keep the 'sir' for when there's brass about or you want to make a point. Otherwise, my name's George. All right?"

"Yes. You George, me Norris," Scobie had said with a grin.

Millson finished fastening the seat belt. "Yes, I know," he said. "But at least it made him tell us about his visit to the house, and the girl."

They interviewed Edward Forman's other daughter, Ruth, in the evening. When they arrived at the house in Coggeshall, it was Quentin Page who opened the door to them this time.

Millson and Scobie followed him along the hall to a door at the far end. "Welcome to our luxury home," he said with heavy sarcasm, opening the door. "This used to be the servants' quarters."

The room was an L-shaped bed-sitting room with a kitchen/diner alcove at one end. At the other end a small bathroom was visible through a half-open door.

Ruth Page rose from an armchair to greet them. Her pale face was sombre and without make-up, and her long dark hair strayed untidily over her face.

"Looks cosy," Millson said, glancing around.

"There's hardly room to swing a cat," Page complained. He pointed to two small kitchen chairs. "You'll have to make do with those, I'm afraid."

He dropped into an upright chair near his wife and watched them sit down, Millson's bulk overlapping the sides of the chair. "All right, Chief Inspector, what d'you want to know?"

Millson eyed him coldly. He recognised the type. A

bumptious know-all. "We've come to interview your wife, Mr Page." He turned his chair towards Ruth Page.

Page bristled. "I suppose you expect me to wait outside in the corridor, do you?"

Millson said over his shoulder, "No, I expect you to keep quiet, Mr Page." Leaning forward he said, "It's Ruth, isn't it?"

"That's right." She had a breathless, eager voice. "This has been a terrible shock to us, Chief Inspector. It's quite dreadful. People at work ask me about the body and I don't know what to say. I keep telling them it's nothing to do with us but it is in a way, isn't it?"

"That's what we're trying to find out," Millson said. "Did you know your brother once called on your aunt and uncle?"

"No, not until he told me on the phone today. He said it was when Mum died. I'd left home and was married by then."

"And now she's back in the same home living like a servant," Page said.

"It's only temporary, Quentin," she said. "They don't want to hear about our troubles."

"Helen was sixteen and she was still living at home, of course," Ruth went on. "She had to more or less take over after Mum died, and look after Bobby and Dad and run the house."

"This feud between your father and his brother Helen mentioned. D'you think your mother knew about it, Ruth?"

"Oh, I'm sure she did, because she once told me Piers and Mary had done something truly awful to Dad. She didn't say what it was but I remember she said it happened before she and Dad met." Ruth Page raised her hands in a gesture of helplessness. "I'm sorry, but that's really all I can tell you."

"Well, thank you anyway," Millson said, and rose to leave.

Quentin Page jumped to his feet. "Is that all, Chief Inspector?" He sounded disappointed.

"Why? Did you want to add anything, Mr Page?" Millson asked.

"Yes. I think you should question Helen closely."

"Quentin!" Ruth's voice was shocked.

"Ruth, I don't think she's been telling the police everything she knows."

"Any reason for thinking that?" Millson asked.

Quentin Page hesitated, then shook his head.

"I'll bear it in mind," Millson said.

"Are you going to question Helen again?" Scobie asked as they drove away.

"Not yet," Millson said. "Have we heard anything from Social Services?"

"Not a thing."

Millson sucked in his cheeks. "Well, I can't wait much longer to go public on Piers and Mary Forman. Give them a ring and stir them up. Remind them this is a murder inquiry and we want to know urgently whether or not this couple had foster children. Now we know there was a girl living there, I'm pretty sure Eddie was right and they did. But I'm not facing the media until I know for sure."

"The girl might have been their daughter, not a foster child," Scobie said.

Millson shook his head. "Eddie said, 'Piers couldn't make babies.' Question is: did they foster a boy as well?"

* * *

The death on Dengie not being due to natural causes, the coroner ordered a post-mortem. There the thick, clinging mud was washed away and it became obvious the man was completely naked. The pathologist's later report to the coroner commented on the fact, and described the body as that of a well-nourished male aged between thirty and forty, with dark hair. He had no injuries and there were no suspicious marks on the body. The cause of death was drowning.

The Maldon police had meanwhile checked the reports of missing persons and, finding none that matched, issued an appeal for information. They believed the man had drowned accidentally and fully expected someone to come forward and claim the body.

Four days later, when there had been no response to Scobie's reminder, Millson told him to get the Director of Social Services on the phone.

"I'm not interested in your staff problems or how many times you've been reorganised!" Millson roared down the phone as the Director began making excuses. "I'm only interested in knowing whether or not Mr and Mrs Forman had foster children in their care. I'm calling a press conference for ten o'clock tomorrow morning, and if I don't have the information by then I'm telling the media your department is obstructing my inquiries!" He slammed down the phone.

"You're bluffing, of course," Scobie said.

"Oh no I'm not," Millson growled.

Jack Belcher had followed the local newspaper and radio reports about the body on Dengie Flats with close interest.

One reporter, who had studied the coastguards' report and the tide tables, had calculated that the man drowned around eleven-thirty. His accompanying photographs pinpointed the site and Jack was excited to discover it was close to where he'd been watching the couple in the car that night.

Jack kept detailed notes of his nocturnal activities in an exercise book. The notes, and his photographic memory, enabled him to recapture the scenes accurately and relive the pleasurable experiences again and again. He usually did his boggling in Maldon, or at the caravan sites around the Blackwater in the holiday season. The Tillingham couple had been a chance discovery, and a satisfying one because of the regularity of their meetings. And now, the pleasure of recalling that particular night would be enhanced by knowing that, as he watched them, nearby a man had been drowning.

He debated whether to tell the police about the boat he saw as he stood on the sea wall with his bike. They might want to know what he was doing there at that time of night, though. Perhaps they had a list of complaints about Peeping Toms in the area, and he would be asked to account for his whereabouts on other nights as well.

Best to keep quiet, Jack Belcher decided.

Seven

The information from the Social Services arrived by fax at nine o'clock the next morning. Five minutes later, as Millson studied it, a WPC brought another fax addressed to him personally. It was from the Director of Social Services complaining about Millson's 'threatening and blackmailing behaviour'. The Director proposed to report it to the Chief Constable unless DCI Millson made an immediate and unreserved apology.

"Tell him to whistle," Millson said, handing it back to the WPC, and resuming his study of the first fax.

The WPC looked anxiously at Scobie. He gave a slight shake of the head, and mouthed, "File it." She nodded and hurried away.

Millson finished reading. He turned to Scobie, his face beaming. "We're in business at last, Norris. Read this. Then get the team together."

The information given by the Social Services department was that three children had been placed with Mary and Piers Forman for fostering when they lived at Wickford in the south of the county. Their names were

Barry Naylor, Alan Stigall and Sandra Mitchell. The first to be placed with them was Barry, when he was nine, followed six years later by Alan, aged thirteen, and Sandra, aged ten. The family later moved to Great Yeldham and shortly before their move, Barry, then sixteen, had absconded. The council had traced him to a hostel, satisfied themselves he was in no danger, and taken no further action. A year after moving to Great Yeldham the Formans reported the other boy, Alan Stigall, had also absconded. Although there was no record he'd been traced, no further action appeared to have been taken about him. The girl, Sandra, had continued living with the Formans and had later been taken off the 'at risk' register. The council had no information about her after that.

There was relief among the Incident Room staff as word spread of a breakthrough. In the month since the body had been found, and an appeal made for information, the staff had been bogged down with missing person inquiries. About a quarter of a million people vanish from home each year without warning, many of them teenagers, and the Incident Room had been swamped with calls from anxious relatives from all over the country. Although most of them could be dismissed because the disappearance was less than twenty years before, the others could not. They had to be logged, and the circumstances of the disappearance and description of the missing person checked in case they matched the youth found at Great Yeldham.

As the inquiries mounted it seemed as if half the teenage population of the country was missing from home. At the same time the staff were attempting to collate the missing person reports from other Forces made between twenty and thirty years ago. Each report had to be followed up to eliminate the ones who'd been accounted for since.

What had depressed Millson was the probability the work was futile because the name of the dead youth would not be found among the missing. He recalled that out of the fifteen youths murdered by Dennis Nilsen in the 1980s, only two had been reported missing.

Now, as the team assembled for the briefing, there was an air of cheerful expectancy. After Scobie had read out the information in the fax, Millson went on:

"The first and most obvious possibility is the body is Alan Stigall's and that Piers, or Piers and Mary together, killed him and buried him, then extended the patio to cover the body. And that's the line we'll follow. On this scenario there are two people who should come forward: the girl, Sandra, and the other boy, Barry Naylor. So we concentrate on finding them. I want our own check carried out on the Social Services records. They should have the names and addresses of the children's natural parents. And check Criminal Records. With their backgrounds it's possible they've been in trouble at some time. The rest of you can start house-to-house enquiries in Yeldham again. The Forman family claim to know nothing about this couple and their foster children but there must be people in the village who knew them."

After the briefing Millson asked the press liaison officer to arrange a full-scale press conference. He wanted maximum coverage given to his information and appeal.

At the meeting with the press Millson informed reporters that the body was now known to have been buried at the time a Piers and Mary Forman were living in the house. The couple died in a car crash five years ago, he went on, and at one time they had fostered three children.

He then repeated in full the information about the children given by the Social Services department. He said he was anxious to trace them and appealed to them to come forward.

A reporter asked if he had made any progress in identifying the skeleton. "Could it be Alan Stigall's?" he asked.

"It's a possibility," Millson said. "We simply don't know at the moment."

Afterwards, when the reporters had left, Scobie asked him if he was now going to question Helen Forman again.

"No, Norris, I'm not," Millson said. "I'll tell you what's going to happen. Now the Press have been told about Piers and Mary Forman and their foster children they'll dig out the rest of the family and turn them over. They'll be looking for stories. That's what they want ... stories. I wouldn't be surprised if one of the tabloids ran one about 'Link found between mystery body under patio and mysterious crash on the M11'. By the way, we'd better check out that crash before some loon suggests it was a suicide or double murder."

Millson pulled a bar of chocolate from his pocket, peeled back the wrapper, and bit off a mouthful. "Now all of this," he said, munching energetically, "will put pressure on the Forman family, particularly on Helen, who's living at the probable scene of the murder. Which means if she's been hiding anything from us, there's a good chance it will come out."

"That's a pretty cynical attitude," Scobie said.

"I know. But much as I dislike the way the media operate, if there's information to be had I'm not fussy how it comes to us."

* * *

On his way to the Cap and Feathers that lunch-time Jack Belcher passed the poster yet again. It was on the noticeboard outside the unmanned police station in Tillingham. The Maldon police, having received no response to their appeal, had posted it on the noticeboard of every police station in the county, together with a photograph of the dead man's face taken at the post-mortem.

There was no other way to the pub and Jack had to pass the DO YOU KNOW THIS PERSON? poster every time he went to the Cap and Feathers, and again on his way home. Every time he passed it his eyes were drawn to the face of the corpse. The man who drowned had meant nothing to Jack when he couldn't put a face to him. Now he could, though, and the gruesome picture haunted him. It was even beginning to intrude on his fantasies when he conjured up memories of the couple in the car.

He knew the only way to rid himself of these intrusions was to unburden his conscience and tell the police what he'd seen that night. But then he'd have to explain what he was doing there, and they would arrest him. Jack Belcher was not a happy person.

"Are you celebrating something, Dad?" Dena asked when Millson opened a bottle of Châteauneuf-du-Pape as they began their evening meal.

"Yes, progress," he said, and gave her a smile.

She nodded and went on with her meal, knowing better than to ask further.

He felt more confident of solving the case now. Social Services had traced Barry after he absconded, and the fourteen-year-old girl Robert Forman saw when he called at the house was almost certainly Sandra. It should be possible to find them unless something had happened to them since. Sandra was the one he most wanted to speak to because she had been living with Piers and Mary Forman at the time the murder occurred.

Reflecting on the time that had been wasted searching through countless missing person reports, Millson recalled a discomforting feature revealed by the reports: almost every young person reported missing had left home without warning, and without a word to anyone. Just upped and gone.

"Why are you staring at me? Have I got a zit on my face or something?" Dena asked suddenly.

He realised he'd been staring at her wondering how he would feel if she went off like that. "Your complexion's fine," he said. "I was wondering about something, that's all. Tell me ... if you were going to leave home would you just up and go? Not even leave a note?"

"If I *what*?"

"If you decided to go off on your own. Would you keep in touch? Let me know you were alive and well?"

She laid down her knife and fork. "Dad ... what *are* you on about? You know I wouldn't do that. Has old Millie been winding you up?"

Millicent Stagg was the fifty-year-old woman who did their housework and shopping, and believed her duties included giving Millson advice about his daughter. The advice invariably came wrapped up in gloom and foreboding.

"No, she hasn't. And you haven't answered the question," he said.

Her forehead creased in a frown as she considered the

matter. "Depends. Not if you turned me out, I wouldn't. I probably wouldn't speak to you ever again."

"Well, I'm not likely to do that, am I?" he said impatiently.

"You might. A fifth-form girl was thrown out by her father last term."

"What for?"

"She was preggers." She saw his expression. "Oh, come on, Dad! I wouldn't be so stupid! Anyway, if I did run off for some reason, I'd keep in touch in case I wanted to come back sometime. It would be silly to cut myself off, wouldn't it?" Her eyebrows came together again. "What's brought this on, if it isn't Millie?"

"We've had mothers and fathers ringing up from all over the place these last few weeks. I didn't realise how many thousands of boys and girls left home without telling anyone."

Her face cleared. "Oh, the body at Great Yeldham," she said brightly, "Jackie says it's the younger boy, and the foster parents must have done it."

"I can do without Jackie Delayney's opinion, thank you," Millson said good-humouredly.

The constable at the inquiry desk in Maldon police station was not interested in Jack Belcher's information at first. After a sleepless night Jack had worked out what he thought would be a suitable excuse for being on the sea wall at that time of night.

"OK, so you saw a boat off Dengie Flats that night. What about it? Those mudflats run for eight miles."

"It were close inshore – near where the body were found."

71

"How could you know that?"

"There meself."

The constable looked at him sharply. "Wait here," he said.

Moments later Jack Belcher found himself in an interview room facing a DC.

"Where *exactly* were you, Mr Belcher?"

"On the sea wall by Marshhouse Outfall."

"What time was this?"

" 'Bout half eleven."

"Uh-huh. And what were you doing there?"

He'd prepared his answer. "I often goes for a walk along the wall after the pubs close. Specially on a fine night near moonrise like it were that night."

The DC nodded. "Tell me about this boat. Can you describe it?"

"She were a yacht … 'bout forty feet … and she were at anchor, but not showing lights."

"Anything else you remember about her?"

"Couldn't see the name, but she had 'Harwich' on the stern."

The DC frowned. "There are marshes beyond the sea wall, aren't there?"

"Yeah."

"And mudflats between them and the sea?"

"Yeah."

"Then, if you were on the wall, as you say, how the hell could you see lettering on a boat at that distance at night?"

Jack had expected them to latch on to that. He daren't mention his binoculars, though. "It were bright moonlight and I had me nightscope with me."

"Your what?"

"Nightscope. It's a kind o' small telescope for seeing in the dark."

The DC's knowledge of infra-red devices for night surveillance was slight, but of one thing he was certain. They were very expensive.

"And what would you be doing with a pricey gadget like that?"

"I uses it to watch wildlife at night. There's otters and all kinds of things around them marshes." He looked the DC in the eye without blinking.

The DC thought Belcher looked anything but a dedicated naturalist, though he couldn't fathom what else he'd be watching in that desolate place. The area was uninhabited, apart from two farmhouses a mile or so away. He let it pass for the moment.

"Pretty powerful is it, this nightscope of yours?"

"Reckon so."

"You didn't see the man trapped in the mud, though?"

"Nope."

"But you think there might be a connection between this yacht you saw, and the man's body being found there?"

"Could be." Jack nodded. It was the reason he'd taken the risk to himself in reporting it. "A boat close inshore there without lights ain't up to no good – 'less it's a winkler, of course, and it weren't."

"What's a winkler?"

Jack gave him a scornful look. These berks in the police knew nothing about what went on around Dengie. No Man's Land it was to them. "A winkler's a winkle-fisherman's boat. Winkle-brigs, they was called in me granddad's time. Don't you know nothink 'bout this area?"

"Oh ... right." Chastened, the DC decided against

enquiring further into Belcher's nightscope or his night-time activities.

Half an hour later Jack Belcher signed a typewritten statement and departed happily, his conscience clear.

After he left, the DC phoned the Immigration Office at Harwich. "A man's body was found on the foreshore at Dengie with no ID," he told an immigration officer. "We've had no one reported missing in the area and now a witness has come forward who says he saw a boat close inshore there the night the body was found. We think you should be informed."

"Too right we should. When was the body found?"

"Eight days ago."

"An unknown turns up on the beach without papers, and you don't tell us for *eight* days? What's with you people?"

"The body was covered in mud and the officers called to the scene thought he was a rambler or hiker who didn't know the area and got caught by the tide. Then when we got the PM report which said he was naked and he'd drowned we assumed he'd been swimming or fallen off a boat. Since then we've been waiting for someone to claim the body."

There was a grunt of impatience on the other end of the phone. "We'll send a man over to view the body, and we'll want the doctor who did the PM to be there. We'll notify Customs and you'd better inform the coroner, and have one of your people there too."

"I don't see why you want us."

"You don't think this man came ashore waving a passport and entry visa and lost them in the mud, do you? That's probably the body of an illegal immigrant who tried to come ashore on Dengie Flats. In which case it'll be your job to find out how he got there."

Eight

The doctor who carried out the post-mortem was irritated to find an immigration officer, a customs officer and a police officer grouped around the body in the examination room.

"I don't know what you're all doing here," he said. "I've made my report and that's all my fee covers. And I'm not qualified in forensic pathology."

The customs officer said, in a placating tone of voice, "We think this man was probably an illegal immigrant, Doctor, and we need your help. Please send your account for this further service to my office."

"Oh, I see." The doctor's face brightened. "Well, how can I help?"

"We understand from your PM report the body was unclothed. Was there no garment of any kind? Briefs? Swim trunks?"

The doctor shook his head. "The body was covered in thick mud and when my assistant washed it clean we discovered it was completely naked. Not a stitch on it."

"This mud that was washed off. Were there any slithers

of paper in it? Or small lumps about the size of shingle?"

Again the doctor shook his head. "My assistant's very thorough. He put the mud, and the muddy water from washing the body, through a fine sieve. It contained nothing but grains of sand."

"Pity," the customs officer said. "You see, these illegals usually carry money or drugs – sometimes precious stones – to pay the people who bring them in, and to help them get started here. Did you look in his back passage?"

The doctor looked startled. "No, I did not! The cause of death was patently obvious to me from an examination of the lungs and airways."

"Do you mind looking now, please?"

Raising his eyebrows, the doctor tore plastic examination gloves from a dispenser, donned them, and turned the corpse on its side. He probed for a while with his fingers then straightened.

"There's nothing there," he said.

"In that case, I want the abdomen X-rayed. He may have been carrying drugs or valuables internally."

The doctor smiled indulgently. "Non-metallic objects won't show up on an X-ray."

The customs officer said patiently, "There's an X-ray technology called xeroradiography available now. It images hard and soft tissue. So it shows up foreign matter … including latex." He smiled thinly. "Useful for spotting swallowed condoms. Perhaps you'd be good enough to ask the forensic laboratory at Huntingdon to do it. They have the equipment. And thank you for your help, Doctor." He turned to the police constable. "Anyone shows up to claim the body, and you phone us at once. OK?"

*   *   *

76

Three days later, when the forensic laboratory's xeroradiographic examination found nothing suspicious secreted in the body, the Customs authorities advised the coroner they had no further interest in it. Soon after this the Rochford District Coroner called the Harwich Chief Immigration Officer, and a police inspector from Maldon, to a meeting in his office.

After reminding them he had a duty under the Coroner's Rules to determine who the deceased was, and how, when, and where, he came by his death, the coroner went on, "All I've been given so far is the date of death and the cause, which was drowning. I have no information on who he was, or on how he came to be drowned. And time is passing." He looked at the police inspector. "What results have you had from your inquiries, Inspector?"

The policeman, a heavy, red-faced man, cleared his throat. "Sir, as to who he was, his body was completely naked and so we have no means of identifying him until someone comes forward with information. We've appealed for information and posted notices and photographs at every police station in the county but, as yet, no one has come forward. We've also checked the missing person reports, of course. As to how he came by his death, there's no evidence of foul play and, bearing in mind the terrain where the body was found, we conclude this was an accident. We think he'd probably been swimming and became trapped in the mud and was drowned by the incoming tide."

"Thank you, Inspector." The coroner turned to the Chief Immigration Officer. "I gather you view this rather differently?"

"I do indeed, sir. We believe the man to be an illegal

immigrant from Eastern Europe, or the Balkans, and this is why no one has reported him missing or come forward with information. Also, we understand a boat was seen near where the body was discovered, which lends further support to our view."

"The boat's just a coincidence," the inspector said. "There are hundred of boats cruising the area at this time of year."

The Chief Immigration Officer ignored the interruption. "There are two possibilities," he said. "One is that the man fell – or was more likely thrown – overboard from a ship entering Felixstowe. Felixstowe is the UK's favourite port of entry for illegal immigrants. The other is that he was landed by small boat. Either way, he was stripped and robbed of his money and possessions, and left to drown. And that's murder. At the very least I think the circumstances are suspicious and should be investigated."

The inspector said curtly, "That's all speculation. It could just as easily be the case that he was naked because he'd been swimming, or because he'd been asleep on a boat and somehow fell overboard."

"Do you mean like Robert Maxwell?" the coroner asked incredulously.

"It's possible, sir," the inspector said, looking hurt.

The coroner was silent for a moment, considering. Then he said, "Inspector, I'm afraid I can't reach a verdict and close this inquest without further investigation."

The inspector looked unhappy. "I'll inform County Headquarters accordingly, sir," he said stiffly.

A check of the Criminal Names Index on the Police National Computer had found no record of Alan Stigall or

Barry Naylor. Sandra Mitchell, however, had several convictions for soliciting in Leeds, the last one five years ago.

"She may still be living there," Millson said. "See if Leeds police have any information about her."

"And Sean Kebble – the boy who went missing the same time as Tom Watson – has been accounted for, sir," a DC said. "His mother phoned Strathclyde police. Apparently Sean made contact with her about ten years after they left Great Yeldham, and he's regularly kept in touch with her ever since. They're sending us a copy of her statement."

"File it," Millson said. "He's of no interest to us now."

The fresh round of inquiries in Great Yeldham had found plenty of people who remembered Piers and Mary Forman and their tragic accident. However, not many of them were living there twenty years ago when the couple and their two foster children first came to the village. Those who were, remembered the fair-haired Sandra well. She had remained with the Formans until well into her teens, they said. The few who could recall Alan Stigall said they had only seen him around for the first two or three years after the family moved there. Everyone who knew them described Piers and Mary Forman as a quiet couple, who looked after the children well, and kept themselves very much to themselves.

The detailed search of the Social Service records by a WDC unearthed an address for Sandra Mitchell's mother, but when detectives visited the address in Rayleigh they found she had moved years ago, and no one knew where she was living now. The WDC also found the address of Barry Naylor's mother, but it turned out to be in a block of flats that had been demolished ten years ago.

There had been no response from any of the fostered

children to the well-publicised appeals, nor had anyone come forward with information about them. Although he told himself it was early days yet, Millson was concerned. He'd expected an early response from at least one of them, which he'd hoped would lead to the identification of the body.

The coroner's request for further investigation of the naked man found drowned on Dengie Flats was passed to Force Headquarters and thence to Colchester Division and Superintendent Kitchen. After a quick glance at the file he sent for Millson.

"Your lad Scobie knows all about boats, they tell me. He's just the man for this job. A man's body on the shore and a mystery boat."

"Hang on a minute," Millson said. "Is this a murder investigation?"

"Ooh no, I shouldn't think so for a minute. There's no evidence of a crime. It's just a matter of tracing a yacht and seeing if it had any connection with the body. Shouldn't take him long." Kitchen held out the file. Millson took it reluctantly. He'd have liked to tell Kitchen the Great Yeldham inquiry was keeping Scobie fully occupied, but it wasn't at the moment.

"By the way," Kitchen said, "I've had a complaint about you passed down to me by the Chief Constable. It's from the Director of Social Services. Seems he wanted an apology and you didn't give him one."

"I didn't think he deserved one, sir."

Kitchen grinned. "My feelings too, George. I'm sending him a soft-soap letter and I don't think we'll hear any more about it."

Millson scanned the report from the Maldon police, then

called Scobie to his room and handed him the file.

"Mr Kitchen thinks this is a job for you, Norris," he said. "Tracing a yacht seen near Dengie Flats. Right up your street, or maybe I should say waterway."

"Why us and not Southend?"

"A witness saw the word 'Harwich' on the stern."

"That doesn't mean she's from this area," Scobie said. "It's simply the original port of registration. She could be based anywhere."

"Yes, but the body was on found on our patch," Millson said. "So take the file away and have a look through it. Then tell me what you think."

Scobie returned a few minutes later. "The first thing is to ask the witness for more details of the boat. But I can't see why the coroner and Immigration people suspect foul play. No one would try to dump a body there. It's too difficult."

"You think so? It's been done before, you know." Millson leaned back in his chair, hands clasped behind his head, and grinned at him.

Scobie recognised the signs. Millson had searched his reference books. At one time, Scobie thought George Millson had an encyclopaedic memory because he always seemed able to cite a previous case similar to the one under investigation. Then Scobie discovered he kept notebooks in his cupboard. labelled *Whatdunit, Wheredunit, Whydunit* and *Whodunit*, which catalogued murders by method, location and motive and enabled him to look for similarities with ease.

"1949 … Stanley Setty," Millson said. "His body was intended to be dumped on those same mudflats. But the killer missed the target and the body ended up floating in the water a couple of hundred yards short in Tillingham Marshes." His face broke in a grin. "Though in that case, of course, the body was clothed, wrapped in a plastic bag, and minus the head and arms."

"What d'you mean, 'the killer missed the target'?"

"The body was dropped from a light aircraft by one Donald Hume. Hume was seen loading two plastic packages into the plane at Elstree, so presumably the second one contained the arms and legs and landed in the mud. Hume was charged with murder but got away with conviction as an accessory. Soon as he'd served his sentence, he admitted the murder and sold his story to the papers."

"No justice," said Scobie.

"Oh, he got his deserts quite soon. A few months later he robbed a bank in Zurich and shot a taxi driver while he was escaping. The Swiss gave him a life sentence, and he was returned to Britain as insane and banged up in Broadmoor."

"But our man wasn't murdered," Scobie said. "There's no evidence of it."

"There's negative evidence, though. No clothes. Did someone strip him? Then throw him overboard expecting the body to sink below the mud and never be found? That's what Hume intended with Setty. He knew the mudflats were used as a bombing range during the war and the mud is like quicksand in places."

"So, you think this man *was* murdered?"

"No, but the coroner doesn't have a satisfactory explanation of how he came to be there without his clothes, and that's why we've been asked to trace the boat."

"That's not going to be easy," Scobie said.

"Superintendent Kitchen has every faith in you, Norris." Millson smiled benignly. "And you'll see from the file Maldon have offered you a DC with local knowledge. Be thankful for small mercies."

*　　*　　*

Scobie was not impressed with DC Tatum when he picked him up at Maldon police station on the way to question Jack Belcher. Tatum was wearing jeans and a black leather jacket. Also, he had dark curly hair and a swarthy face which made him look more like a gypsy than a detective. Scobie, who always wore a suit on duty, felt uncomfortable with him. However, Tatum was said to know the Dengie area well and Scobie needed his knowledge.

It was midday when they arrived in Tillingham, and Scobie decided to have lunch in the local pub before interviewing Belcher. Their entry to the Cap and Feathers provoked sideways glances from the men sitting at the bar, hunched over their glasses.

"Natives look a bit unfriendly," Scobie said as they settled themselves at a table with their beers and a plate of roast pheasant sandwiches.

"Grub's good, though." Tatum clamped his jaws on a sandwich, tore a section off and chewed appreciatively.

"DCI Millson doesn't think this man drowned by accident," Scobie said, cutting his sandwich in half with a knife. "He suggests he was thrown overboard here because his killer didn't want the body to be found. Like the Setty case fifty years ago."

Bill Tatum's face lit up. "Ah … Stanley Setty."

"You know the case?" Scobie was surprised.

Tatum grinned. "Not half. So does everyone round here. The punt-gunner who found him lived in Tillingham and he only died a couple of years back. That kind of story gets passed on and never dies. 'Specially in the pub here. This is where they brought Setty's body."

"Really?" Scobie looked around with interest.

"Oh, not to the bar, Sarge. It's against the law to hold a

post-mortem on licensed premises. They took him to a shed at the back and did the autopsy there. This whole area was buzzing with journalists for months after. Even today we sometimes get some writer or crime reporter snooping around." Tatum paused to take a large mouthful of beer. "Anyway, no disrespect to the DCI, but I don't reckon this guy was murdered. I reckon he was an illegal immigrant who was dead unlucky."

"Apparently, the Immigration people think so too," Scobie said.

"Course they do. They've got them flooding in at the moment. Hiding in ship's lifeboats … hanging underneath lorries … sealed up in containers. Last December, Customs found fifteen hiding in a consignment of Christmas trees on the back of a lorry."

"But crawling up the mudflats here is a bit unlikely, isn't it?" Scobie said.

"Oh no, not at all, Sarge. It's isolated … hardly anyone lives here … and there's an eight-mile stretch of completely deserted coast. What's more, Southminster station is less than three miles away and you can be in Liverpool Street in an hour and a quarter. All the guy needs is a sketch map of the area and money for the fare and a phone call."

"Phone call?"

"For someone to meet him at Liverpool Street and whisk him away to a safe refuge. He'll have been given a contact in this country."

Scobie regarded him keenly. "You seem to know a lot about it."

Tatum shrugged. "I was born in Burnham-on-Crouch and I've lived in and around this area all my life."

Nine

Jack Belcher was startled to find two police officers on his doorstep so soon after his visit to Maldon police station. He came out quickly on to the front step and pulled the door to behind him.

"Let's go somewhere else to talk. I don't want my nosy landlady asking questions."

"In the car, then?" Scobie suggested.

"Yeah, but not outside here." Jack Belcher jerked his head. "Drive down the road a bit."

As he drove out of Tillingham, with its neat white-painted weatherboard houses, Scobie said, "I'd like to take a look at where you were that night, so we'll drive on and do the talking there. Tell me where to go."

"Oh, I wouldn't do that," Belcher said. "Folks round here are funny about strangers. They're likely to take pot shots at you and pretend they was shooting ducks."

"We're police officers!" Scobie said.

Jack Belcher grinned. "They wouldn't know that, would they? And anyways, coppers rate same as Customs in these parts. And *they* has the sense to come armed."

Scobie stopped the car. "I don't believe I'm hearing this," he said.

In the passenger seat DC Tatum muttered from the side of his mouth, "This is bandit country, Sarge. Smuggling."

Scobie stared at him in disbelief. "I still want to see exactly where he was standing when he saw the boat," he said.

In the seat behind him Belcher made a face. "Orlright, then. But you'd best let me give Ray Powers a bell first. It's his land you 'as to cross an' he looses off his shotgun at people he don't know. Turn left along the road here. There's a phone box by Grange Farm."

Twenty minutes later the three of them had scrambled up the twenty-foot-high earthworks that formed the sea wall and walked along it to where Belcher had stood with his bike.

Scobie gazed in awe at the vast wilderness. Immediately below them the marshes, covered with sea lavender and glasswort, stretched up and down the coast as far as the eye could see. Beyond the marshes were miles of mudflats that eventually met a distant sea.

"My God," he said. "This must be one of the loneliest places in the whole country. I never imagined it was like this."

"Nothing here 'cept birds and wild duck," Belcher said.

"Where was the boat?" Scobie asked.

Belcher raised his arm and pointed. "She were anchored there. Tide were half up then, so water were a lot closer." He swung his arm in an arc and pointed to a shallow trough that ran seawards through the channels and swatchways of the marsh. "An' that's Marshhouse Outfall where the poor sod sank in the mud and drowned."

Scobie swept his eyes over the mudflats. "If he did come

off that yacht, he'd have been lucky to make it to the sea wall at night."

"Suicide to even try it without splatchers," said Belcher. "Only safe place to land is up at Bradwell on Sales Point. Or else down the other end of the Flats at Holliwell Point."

"You didn't give much description of this yacht in your statement. What did she look like?"

"Well, she weren't some old gaffer, I c'n tell you. She were a classy-looking job."

"That the best you can do?"

"No." Belcher sounded offended and closed his eyes. "She were about forty feet ... sloop-rigged ... sails stowed ... a radar blister foreside of the masthead ... centre cockpit ... white hull and topsides ... and a kind of cutaway stern." He opened his eyes.

"That's very good," Scobie said. "You must have a photographic memory."

"Yeah, I have ... sort of." Jack Belcher smirked. It was his knack of total recall that enabled him to reproduce the sex scenes so accurately.

"Think you could draw me a silhouette – an outline of her shape?"

"Reckon so."

Scobie gestured to Tatum to hand his notebook and pen to Belcher. Belcher turned to a blank page, carefully drew a shape on it, and passed the notebook to Scobie.

Scobie studied the drawing. "That's great," he said returning the book to Tatum.

The DC peered at the drawing. "Can't tell anything from that, can you?"

"Yes. That retroussé stern is quite distinctive."

"That *what* stern?"

"Retroussé. That's the yacht designers' fancy name for a short, turned-up stern. In modern yachts it serves as a bathing platform. It will help identify her."

"Better if he'd taken the name, if you ask me," Tatum said.

"Didn't have no name," Belcher said. "Just some letters and figures."

"You mean like a fishing boat?"

"No, course not. SSR something."

"SSR? You saw the letters SSR?" Scobie asked eagerly.

"Yeah."

"Then she's on the Small Ships Register," Scobie said with mounting interest. "Did you see the figures? There would have been figures after the letters."

Belcher pursed his lips, hesitated, and shook his head.

"Try hard, Jack," Tatum said. "Else we might have to look into what you was doing here that time of night."

Belcher looked at him fearfully and closed his eyes again. First, he had to visualise the sex scene. That was the key that unlocked his subconscious and triggered a trance-like state of total recall. It was nearly half a minute before he opened his eyes and said, "Three figures. One ... five ... and something. I didn't get the last figure."

Scobie stared at him open-mouthed. "How on earth do you do that?"

"Jus' a knack I has." He was looking anxiously at Tatum.

Tatum grinned at him. "Happy hunting, Jack," he said, and winked.

"What was going on between you two?" Scobie asked after they had dropped Belcher. (Belcher had asked to be put down some distance from his house. "I don't wanna be seen with you two. People might think I've bin nicked.")

"Jack's a Peeper, Sarge," Tatum said. "Everyone in the village knows it, but he pretends they don't. I'm surprised he found any boggling to do round here, though."

Passing Scobie's door next morning Millson saw him turning the pages of a magazine. Other magazines and brochures were piled on his desk. Millson sauntered in, picked one off the pile and idly turned the pages. He stopped at a glossy advertisement, eyebrows raised.

"A hundred and twenty-five *thousand*?" he said, shaking his head in disbelief. "Is that what these things cost? I could buy a house for that."

"It wouldn't sail very well, though," Scobie said.

"Never mind the funnies, Norris. Just explain to me why anyone would use a sailing boat for smuggling."

"These aren't sailing boats, they're yachts," Scobie said crossly. "They're more suitable than motor cruisers for long sea journeys and the one you're looking at has a fifty-horsepower Volvo engine."

"OK, no need to get shirty. Have you traced this one? I take it that's the point of all this reading and you're not contemplating buying one?"

"I haven't found her yet. But I've got a good description and she's registered with the Department of Trade's Small Ships Register. Unfortunately, the witness only remembers part of the number so I'm trying to identify her marque and class."

"That sounds like trying to trace a car with only half the registration number and without knowing the make."

"It's not like that at all," Scobie said peevishly. "The register was only started five years ago and not all vessels are on it, whereas there are something like fourteen million cars on the vehicle registration index. Also there aren't that many yachts fitting the description given by the witness."

"Hopeful of a quick result, then, are you?"

"Very," Scobie said.

Millson nodded. "Good for you. Wish I could say the same for the Great Yeldham case."

Half an hour later Scobie was confident the yacht was either a Moody 38 or a Westerly Oceanlord 41. He phoned the Small Ships Registry at Swansea and asked them to fax him details of the vessels on the register with SSR numbers 150 to 159, and the names and addresses of their owners.

When the reply came he gave a whoop of delight. It had been easier than he expected. Of the ten vessels listed there was only one Moody 38 and it was registered to a Gregory Henderson living in London.

Next day Scobie had to pass through an elaborate security check in the entrance hall before he was allowed to take a lift to the sixteenth floor of the block of flats in the Barbican.

"Mr Henderson?"

"Yes." The blond man who answered the door nodded.

Scobie identified himself for a second time and repeated the explanation he'd given over the intercom. "I'm carrying out a routine check on entries in the Department of Trade's Small Ships Register, Mr Henderson. May I come in?"

"Sure."

Stepping inside, Scobie covertly appraised the flat. He noted a Harrods stainless steel fridge-freezer that would have cost all of two thousand pounds, as he passed the door of the galley-type kitchen. The suite in the lounge, where they took seats, was black leather and through the window he had a view of the dome of St Paul's.

"Nice view, isn't it?" Henderson said, following the direction of his gaze.

A flat in a luxury block in the Barbican ... an expensive yacht ... financed perhaps by smuggling illegal immigrants into the country? "Expensive, too, I imagine," Scobie said casually.

Henderson laughed. "Oh, the flat's not mine. It goes with my job ... same as the car."

"What job is that?"

"I'm a market trader for a City finance house."

Which might or might not be true, Scobie thought. "I believe you own a Moody 38 yacht called the *Lady Madonna*. She's registered on the Small Ships Register."

"Yes, that's right."

"Do you hold British citizenship? Only British citizens can register their yachts."

"Yes, of course. D'you want to see my passport?"

"No, that won't be necessary. And was your vessel previously registered at Harwich?"

"Yes, as a matter of fact, she was."

That clinched matters for Scobie. He asked casually, "Do you mind telling me where the vessel was on the night of the twenty-first of June?"

Henderson raised his eyebrows. "Why d'you want to know?" He looked hard at Scobie. "Look, what's this about? It's not about the yacht register at all, is it? What's the significance of the twenty-first of June?"

"A yacht answering her description was seen lying off Dengie Flats at the time a man drowned there."

"So?"

"The man was an illegal immigrant."

"*What?*" Henderson's eyes widened.

"Now perhaps you'll tell me where your boat was that night."

Henderson shrugged his shoulder. "I don't know. When I said I own the *Lady Madonna*, that's not strictly true. I bought her with a whacking great marine mortgage, and couldn't keep up the payments. The finance company were about to repossess her when I spotted an advert in *Yachting Monthly* that seemed the answer to my prayers. It's a scheme whereby you sell a share in your yacht to a charter company and they let it out on charter, and pay you a percentage of the income. That's what I did, and the company paid off my mortgage with the finance company. So now they let her out on charter from April to September, and I have use of her from October to March. It's a very good deal. I have no hand in the chartering so I've no idea where she was or who had her in June."

Scobie hid his disappointment. "Where is this charter company?"

"Kirby-le-Soken near Walton on the Naze. It's owned by Bobby Forman."

Scobie frowned. "*Robert* Forman?"

"Yes, d'you know him?" Henderson's mouth dropped open. "Jesus! Of course you do. You're from the *Essex* police ... the skeleton at his sister's place! Is there some connection with my yacht?"

There is now, Scobie thought, and the sooner I report it to Millson the better. He smiled reassuringly. "Not that we know of, Mr Henderson. This is a separate inquiry I'm engaged on, and thank you for your help."

Ten

Scobie had expected Millson to want Robert Forman interviewed straight away, but when he phoned him Millson said, "Leave it till the morning, Norris, and we'll tackle him together. I'm seeing Helen Forman this evening. The publicity is getting her down."

Helen Forman had been upset when she phoned Millson earlier. The cool, competent nurse, unmoved by blood and skeletons, sounded on the verge of tears.

"The phone never stops ringing ... and they're lying in wait when I leave for work. It's terrible," she wailed.

"You mean reporters?"

"Reporters ... photographers ... television people. They're all convinced my aunt and uncle were murderers."

At his desk, Millson nodded. It was what he'd expected.

"I'm nothing to do with all this. I'm an innocent party," Helen said. "Can't you do something?"

"Suppose we discuss it over a drink after work."

"Yes, all right. Where?"

"The Red Lion? Say six o'clock?"

"I'll be there," she said.

He nearly missed her when he entered the bar. He'd been expecting her in uniform. Instead, she was wearing a sleeveless summer dress.

"It's sweltering hot," she said as they carried their drinks outside to a table in Red Lion Walk. "I don't know how you manage in a suit this weather."

"I don't. I take off the jacket – and the tie – and undo the shirt," he said, carrying out the actions as he spoke.

Her worried face broke into a smile. "Does this mean you're off duty?"

"I'm afraid not." He sat down. "I want to know what you're keeping from me about your aunt and uncle."

The smile vanished and her face registered shock. "Quentin, I suppose," she said bitterly. "It's not important."

"Let me decide that," Millson said.

"Is this the price I have to pay for your help?" Her voice was brittle.

"It's what you have to do to gain my confidence," he said.

She gave him a long look before she spoke again. "Well, it's nothing sinister. It's simply very personal to my dad and something he didn't want people to know about. When he told it me he trusted me to keep it secret. And now he's helpless and you can't force him to speak, you want to drag it out of *me*. That's not very nice."

"I hear a lot of family secrets in my job. I'm very good at keeping them," he said.

"That won't stop me feeling guilty. You ought to feel guilty too, prying into my father's private world." When he didn't respond she gave him a disparaging look and went on, "Piers and Mary did something quite dreadful to Dad. You see, Mary was his childhood sweetheart and he was very much in love with her. They were very young ... and they were getting married. On the wedding day …" She paused. "It was like a Victorian melodrama. There was my father sitting in the church in his morning-coat … his best man beside him … the congregation behind … waiting for his bride. Then one of the ushers comes hurrying down the aisle and whispers to him. His brother, Piers, *his own brother*, has run off with her."

Helen Forman picked up her drink and took a mouthful. "Can you imagine what that did to him? It broke him completely. He told me he couldn't speak to anyone for weeks. After that, he cut them out of his life. Later, he married Mum, and then we came along. But he would never speak about them, and he made sure we never met them. He only told me about them when they were dead. And even then he didn't tell Christine. He never got over the hurt, you see." Her eyes were moist. "So, there you are. That's what you wanted to know."

"Yes, and thank you for telling me, Helen."

Millson was thoughtful. Eddie Forman had burnt their possessions … destroyed every trace of them … venting years of pent-up rage on all that was left of the pair who betrayed him. He must have been harbouring that rage for fifty years. Had he never tried to trace them? Never confronted them?

Helen Forman broke in on this thoughts. "Are you going to arrest me for withholding information?"

"No. No, I'm satisfied what you've told me has no bearing on my investigation."

She gave a mocking laugh. "You sound just like a policeman being interviewed on television."

"Well, I would, wouldn't I?" Millson snapped.

"I'm sorry, I didn't mean to be rude," she said contritely.

"Look, I've told you what you wanted to know. So, please can you stop those reporters harassing me?"

"I'll get our press liaison officer to have a word with their editors," Millson said. "She's good at frightening them off. They need our cooperation more than we need theirs, so you shouldn't have any more trouble."

"Thank you. Am I allowed to buy you a drink?"

"Thanks, but I have to get home."

"Wife waiting?" she asked lightly.

"Worse," he said. "Teenage daughter."

She laughed. She was relaxed, off her guard. Keeping his voice level, Millson asked casually, "I wonder how your father knew Piers and Mary had foster children?"

She blinked her eyes. "I imagine someone must have told him," she said.

"You don't think he might have visited them at some time?"

"No, I'm sure he didn't."

He saw her eyes flick away from him. She was lying. Pity. He liked Helen.

Robert Forman's boatyard was at the end of a lane leading from Kirby-le-Soken to the Walton Backwaters. Like many East Coast boatyards it was at the head of a tidal inlet. The deep-water moorings were in Kirby Creek and Hamford Water.

At the side of the inlet was a large shed of corrugated sheeting, painted dark red, with a slipway from its open end to the water. Nearby were two smaller sheds with timber stacked against their sides, where traditional wooden dinghies were built. In front of the sheds, a concrete apron extended into a small quay with another slipway beside it.

A tractor stood at the top of the slipway, its towing chain leading down the slipway to a cradle under the water.

When Millson drove in through the yard entrance and parked, a deep-keeled yacht had been floated into the cradle and began rising from the water as the tractor slowly hauled the cradle up the slipway. Scobie watched in fascination as the vessel rose higher and higher until it came to rest towering above them on its eight-foot keel.

"You're doing it again, Norris," Millson said jokingly.

"Doing what?"

"Drooling. The way you were drooling over the yachts in those photographs at Forman's house. Like they were pin-ups. Yachts affect you that way, do they? And I thought you were a dinghy sailor."

"I am. But I can dream, can't I?"

"Not while you're on duty," Millson said with a grin. He stepped out of the car. "Come on."

They made for a long wooden shed with a board on the side which read: *Forman & Co. Yacht Charters & Moorings*. Before they reached it, Robert Forman emerged looking surprised. "What brings you here, Chief Inspector?"

"We're interested in a yacht called the *Lady Madonna*. Hasn't Mr Henderson told you?"

"Yes, but I was expecting a visit or a phone call from the local police. If I'd known you were coming, I could have saved you a journey."

"How's that?"

"Well, there's obviously been a mistake. I've checked our booking ledger. The *Lady Madonna* wasn't on charter on the twenty-first of June when she was supposed to have been seen at Dengie. She was here in the yard being

97

repaired. The previous hirer ran into a buoy and damaged the pulpit. So there's no way it could have been the *Lady Madonna* off Dengie Flats that night. There are other Moody 38s in the area, you know."

Scobie said, "Not registered with the Small Ships Register and with the same number as the *Lady Madonna* there aren't, Mr Forman."

Forman shrugged. "Well, all I can tell you is this one was up on the hard here on that date. Perhaps you'd like to come inside and look at the booking ledger for yourself."

They followed him into the shed and to the far end where there was a small office without a door. The shed was lined with shelves containing tins of paint, blocks, boxes of bolts and shackles, and general chandlery.

Forman ducked into the office and picked up a ledger lying on the desk there. "I left it open at the page," he said, passing the ledger to Scobie. "You'll see the previous hire period ended on the nineteenth of June and the next one didn't start until the twenty-sixth."

Scobie studied the entries on the page headed LADY MADONNA. He'd hoped they would look fresh – made after Henderson had phoned Forman. The ink looked old, however, and against the week the nineteenth to twenty-sixth of June was written, 'Under repair'. He handed the ledger back. "Perhaps we could have a word with the yard foreman," he said.

"What for? Don't you believe me?" Forman's tone was truculent.

It was Millson who answered. "We don't take anything on trust when we're investigating a murder, Mr Forman."

"*Murder?*" Forman's face paled. "I understood the man drowned."

"Oh, he drowned all right," Millson said. "But throwing him overboard, or deliberately putting him ashore on dangerous mudflats, is murder in my book."

"Oh ... yes." Robert Forman looked worried. "I'll call him." He lifted a microphone from a hook on the wall. "Steve! Can you come to the office for a moment. There are two police officers here asking about the *Lady Madonna*."

Several moments later a thick-set man with a shaved head, and wearing blue overalls, entered the shed. "What's up?" He stared at Millson and Scobie.

"We're interested in the whereabouts of the yacht on the night of the twenty-first of June," Millson said.

"Like it says in the book, she was out of commission that week," Steve Gumbrell said. "Up here in the yard."

Scobie realised Forman must have discussed it with him before they arrived. "Where is she now?" he asked.

"On her mooring in Hamford Water."

"Anyone else work here?"

"Only old Aubrey. He's part-time," Gumbrell said.

As Scobie was considering another question, Millson said, "Looks as though the *Lady Madonna* is ruled out, then. Thank you both. That's all." He nodded to the two men then turned and went out.

Following after him to the car, Scobie said in an aggrieved tone, "That *must* be the yacht ... everything fits. Why are we leaving?"

Millson opened the car door. "So they'll think we've accepted their story. Why are you so sure that's the yacht?"

Scobie reached into the passenger seat and opened his case. "I've got all the guff here. Brochures ... fax from Swansea and—"

"Not here, Norris! They'll see. Where's the nearest pub?"

"The Ship in Kirby."

As Millson drove back along the lane Scobie asked, "What did Helen Forman have to say yesterday evening?"

"She explained what the feud was between Eddie and his brother. Seems the brother ran off with Eddie's bride on the wedding day."

"That must have been pretty devastating for him," Scobie said. "What did Eddie do?"

"According to Helen he simply cut them out of his life. But I wonder if he might have taken revenge in some way."

"Surely not killed one of their foster children, though?" Scobie asked.

"No, of course not. But Helen's keeping something back. Something about her father. I'm sure of it."

When they reached the Ship they took their drinks outside and sat in the garden. Scobie opened his case and lifted the contents on to the table.

"No nautical jargon, Norris. Just the facts," Millson said.

"Yes, OK. The witness described the yacht as sloop-rigged, about forty feet long, with a centre cockpit and scooped stern. And he drew an outline of it. Now, the only two yachts that fit all those features are a Westerly Oceanlord and a Moody 38. Take a look at these pictures of them."

Millson leaned forward as Scobie unfolded two brochures and then reiterated the description, pointing to the feature in each photograph as he did so.

When he'd finished, Millson said. "There must be lots of these boats, though."

"Ah, but what clinches the *Lady Madonna* is the SSR number."

"Your witness made a mistake in the number, then,"

Millson said bluntly. "You said he could only remember part of it."

"He saw three figures and he was certain the first two were one and five," Scobie said. "So I asked Swansea for details of yachts with registration numbers one hundred and fifty to one hundred and fifty-nine. The only Moody 38 is the *Lady Madonna* owned by Henderson."

Millson pursed his lips. "Why didn't the witness see the name?"

"Perhaps it was covered over," Scobie said.

"And this SSR number left showing? No, it has to be another boat of the same type with a false number."

Scobie frowned. "That would mean someone just happened to choose the number of the *Lady Madonna*, which happens to be the same class as the mystery yacht, and also happens to be berthed in this area. That's too many coincidences.

"And there's another thing," he went on. "Those photographs you said I was leering at on Forman's wall. Several of them were Moody 38s. I'll bet Forman has other Moody 38s besides the *Lady Madonna* on his books. I think we should go back and question him further."

"All right, but not yet, Norris. He strikes me as the worrying sort. Give him a ring and tell him we have more questions. But make the appointment for next week. That'll give him time to worry."

Robert Forman told his wife he'd had a visit from the police when she came home from work that evening. Fenella commuted daily to the City and was often late getting home. He'd already had his evening meal.

"What did they want?" She sounded uninterested as she

began preparing a meal for herself.

"They wanted to know where the *Lady Madonna* was on the night of the twenty-first of June."

She laughed. "Sounds as though they suspect her of committing a crime."

"It's Greg Henderson's boat." He watched her for a reaction.

"Yes, I know." She turned and gazed at him steadily until he dropped his eyes.

Fenella relaxed. He didn't suspect. She already knew the police were asking questions about the *Lady Madonna*. Greg had told her. She had spent an hour in bed with him before catching her train home.

Eleven

Fenella had met Greg Henderson two months earlier after he replied to an advertisement her husband had placed in one of the yachting magazines. It was Fenella herself who suggested the advertisement. The yard was losing money, and Bobby had been complaining about rising costs and the lack of capital to buy another yacht for charter.

"Ask your father for another loan, then," Fenella suggested.

"You know he's not well, Fen. He wouldn't know what I was talking about."

"Then go and sweet-talk Christine. I'm sure she'll coax it out of him for you like she did before."

"Leave Christine out of this, please."

"Why?" Fenella's tone was mocking. "Don't you usually go running to her when you want something? Your trouble is you've never grown up, Bobby. You've been looking for a mother ever since your mum died and Christine fills the part nicely."

"Don't be ridiculous!" he said angrily. "Anyway, Dad

103

doesn't have that sort of money to spare. We're talking two hundred grand, for God's sake!"

"So, are you going to sit on your backside and let the business go under, then?"

"I don't see what I can do."

"Oh, don't be so wet!" His lack of initiative infuriated her. "Why don't you do what other charter companies do? Advertise for owners who want to make money chartering their boat, but haven't the facilities to do it themselves. That's what I'd do if it were my business."

"I suppose we could try that," he said doubtfully.

"You'll need good presentation," she said. "So let *me* handle it. After all, it's what I do at work every day."

He'd agreed, and she'd drafted the advertisement for him. Greg Henderson had answered and after an exchange of phone calls Fenella had set up a meeting.

She brought a set of chairs and a table from home and arranged them in the shed. She laid out the table with notepads, pens and pencils, and bottles of mineral water and made Bobby and Steve Gumbrell wear suits.

When Greg Henderson sailed the *Lady Madonna* into Hamford Water and dropped anchor, Fenella had already found out the yacht was heavily mortgaged and Henderson was having difficulty keeping up the payments.

He came ashore in a runabout and seemed impressed by the yard and the arrangements made for the meeting. It was also clear to Fenella he was interested in loaning his yacht for charter, and she was confident of doing a deal with him.

The discussions soon began to falter, though, and she realised he was put off by Bobby's hesitant manner. There had been other advertisements like theirs in the yachting press that month, and she was afraid Greg Henderson would leave and offer his yacht elsewhere.

So far, she had left the discussions to the three men, and confined herself to taking notes. Now, as Henderson seemed to be losing interest, she quickly intervened.

"We'd really love to have the *Lady Madonna*, Mr Henderson," she said earnestly. "And I can promise you we'll look after her as though she were our own boat."

His blue eyes switched to her. She met his gaze frankly as he appraised her. His eyes roamed over the raven hair, cut helmet-style with the ends turned under to caress the cheeks, took in her full red lips, lingered briefly, then rose to meet hers again. Her eyes were an unusual blue-green colour and he wondered if she wore coloured contact lenses.

Still staring into them, he said to Robert Forman, "OK, it's a deal."

Later, when the paperwork had been made out and signed, he said ruefully, "I guess now I have to take the train home."

"I'll run you to the station," Fenella said.

In the car, he'd wasted no time. "What's a lovely creature like you doing in a backwater like this?" he asked, putting his hand on her knee.

"I get my kicks in town during the week, thank you," she said, taking a hand off the wheel, and firmly removing his as it moved up her thigh.

He laughed. "Where do you work?"

She told him.

The next morning he phoned her at work and invited her to lunch. By the afternoon they were in bed together at his flat. She'd been his mistress ever since.

*   *   *

Following Millson's instructions, Scobie phoned Robert Forman on Wednesday, the day after their visit, and made an appointment to see him the following Monday. Later on Wednesday, a copy of Tracey Kebble's statement to the Strathclyde police arrived. It contained information the Scottish police hadn't mentioned on the phone.

"I know you said file it, sir," said the DC who brought it to Millson, "but I think you'll want to see it first."

The statement revealed that when the teenaged Sean had deserted his mother years before in Great Yeldham, he'd only gone as far as Wickford. Unaware of this, Tracey Kebble had moved to Scotland believing she'd never see him again. It had been ten years before he got in touch with her, and then only to borrow money. Over the years Sean had continued to show up at intervals but it was only recently he'd told her he and Barry Naylor had been friends when the two of them lived in Wickford. Later, when Barry absconded from the Formans just before they moved to Great Yeldham, he'd lived in the same hostel as Sean.

"I want Sean Kebble found," Millson told his team as he gave them the information. "He could have important information about the Formans and why none of their foster children have come forward. Put out a new appeal for him and ask Strathclyde to interview the mother again. She must have some idea where he is."

In the two months since they met, the relationship between Fenella and Greg Henderson had developed into an obsession. They snatched moments together at every opportunity ... lunch-time ... the evening, before she caught her train home ... sometimes even in the morning before she went to work. Never at weekends, though, and

Fenella found the weekends hard to bear. So, when Bobby told her he would be busy at the yard this weekend, she pricked up her ears.

"Doing what?" she asked.

"The police are coming on Monday to ask more questions. I'm going to go through the books and list the names and addresses of everyone we've hired a boat to this season. And I'm also going to check the log of every yacht that was on hire the week that body was found on Dengie."

"Poor lamb, you *are* going to be busy." Her mind was already working out how she could meet Greg without arousing suspicion.

By Thursday evening she had made her plan. As she began putting her clothes back on in Greg's flat, she said, "There's no booking for the *Lady Madonna* next week. Come down and spend the weekend on her."

From the bed Greg said lazily. "And tease myself with being close to you? I'd go nuts."

"Bobby's going to be busy at the yard all weekend. Sail her round to Mistley and I'll join you there."

"Sounds a bit risky."

"It isn't. It's only a mile from Manningtree, and I could get back to the house in minutes if I had to." Her eyes were bright. "I want you, Greg. I *need* you."

He smiled. "Why don't you leave him and get a divorce?"

"Because, my sweet, if we divorce I lose the chance of taking over the business. It could make real money if it was handled properly," Fenella said, pulling up her tights.

"But the only way you'll get your hands on it is if Bobby dies."

"That's right," she said, watching his face.

He sat up, his eyes meeting hers. "Are you thinking what I think you're thinking?"

"Probably," she said, holding her gaze steady. When he continued looking at her, a curious, amused expression on his face, she went on eagerly, "Oh, Greg, darling, we'd make a great partnership. We'd turn the business into a howling success, I know we would."

"We'd never get away with it."

She felt a surge of relief. He hadn't shied away, hadn't so much as flinched. "It would have to be an accident," she said.

"What d'you have in mind?"

She shrugged. "Drowning, perhaps. Suppose he banged his head and slipped overboard from a boat, unconscious."

"Somebody would have to hit him hard on the head first."

"Well, obviously," she said impatiently. "Look, if you're not up to it, say so now and we'll forget it."

"It's not that. It's difficult to fake that kind of accident. He might put up a fight and then there'd be suspicious marks on him."

"Well, suppose we got him drunk, and you held his head under water until he drowned, and then we dropped him overboard?"

He raised his eyebrows and smiled crookedly. "You really hate the poor bugger, don't you?"

"No, but he makes me cringe every time he touches me and I can't stand him. I want him gone, Greg."

"You still go to bed with him, though."

"Not often, darling, and only to keep him from suspecting."

"Beats me how you do it."

"I think of you while he's screwing me, that's how," she said, pulling the neck of her dress down over her head and shaking her hair free. "What about a fire? Bobby's always carrying on about the risks with bottled gas on boats."

"That's a possible," he said. "So long as we could be sure he didn't survive."

On Friday evening Millson returned home to find his daughter preening herself in front of the hall mirror.

"Where are you off to?" he asked.

"There's a disco at the Walton yacht club."

"That's a long way to go for a disco. What are you doing for transport?"

"Jackie's father's taking us. He's a member of the yacht club and he's helping with the disco."

"H'm. I s'pose that's all right." He was amazed that Delayney *père* was not only on hand for once, he was carrying out paternal duties.

Dena sidled up to him and picked a hair from his lapel. "I'll be home by half one," she said.

He grunted. "Make sure you are."

A heavy mist rose over Hamford Water as darkness fell that evening and the lingering heat of a warm day met the cold surface of the water. Near the entrance to Kirby Creek, a light showed on board the *Lady Madonna* where Robert Forman was working below in the engine compartment.

Through the mist an inflatable dinghy, with its outboard canted from the water, was being quietly rowed towards the moored yacht. Nearing the yacht, the occupant shipped the oars and, lying prone over the inflatable's bow, paddled with his hands as the tide carried him silently to the stern of the *Lady Madonna*. Reaching up, he grasped the yacht's rail to prevent the dinghy bumping the hull. Securing the dinghy's painter to a cleat, he hauled himself quietly aboard the yacht.

Robert Forman looked up, startled, as he heard feet descending the steps into the saloon. He scrambled out of the engine compartment and turned to find himself confronted by a hooded figure. The hand was pointing a Verey signalling pistol at him, the loaded flare cartridge clearly visible.

He raised his arms automatically. "Who—? What do you want?"

The man put a finger to the slit in the hood where his mouth showed, commanding silence. With a jerk of the pistol he signalled Bobby to move to the centre of the saloon.

Bobby Forman had heard about the trade in stolen yachts. They were sailed across the Channel to some disreputable boatyard, spray-painted a different colour, and given a new name. Within hours they would be on their way to the Mediterranean with false papers and either sold or put out to charter. It was a lucrative business, bringing the thieves a handsome reward for a few hours' work.

"If you want to steal the yacht, just take her and put me off in the dinghy," he said.

Without answering, the man signalled him to turn round. His hands were yanked behind him and he felt cord being tied round his wrists. "There's no need for this!" he cried. "I'm not going to—"

"Shut up!" the man snarled, forcing him to his knees.

Taking a roll of parcel tape and a knife from his pocket, he cut off a strip of tape and stretched it over Bobby's mouth. Then he cut a second piece and knelt down beside him. Wrapping an arm round his shoulders, he held him tight and pressed one end of the tape onto his cheek. Then, with a quick movement, he pulled the tape across Bobby's nose and secured the end to his other cheek. As he bucked and reared the man moulded the tape over the nostrils with his fingers, shutting off the air supply.

He stood up and watched his victim topple forward on the floor, jerking and kicking as he suffocated.

When the movements ceased the man waited a moment or two longer then bent over the body and removed the tape from the face and the cord from the wrists. Dragging the body to the engine compartment, he humped it over the cylinder block.

He pulled a plastic bag from his pocket and took out the hanks of cord that had been soaked in a mixture of diesel oil and petrol. He'd made several tests to arrive at the mix of fuel that would burn slowly and steadily. He laid the cord along the floor of the saloon, into the engine compartment, and up through an air vent to the floor of the cockpit above.

Moving back to the saloon and along to the galley, he filled a kettle with water, placed it on the stove, and turned the gas tap a quarter on. Then, mounting the steps to the cockpit, he took out a cigarette lighter and kneeling down, lit the end of the fuel-soaked cord where it emerged through the ventilator.

For a second or two he watched it burn. From the tests, he'd calculated the flame creeping slowly along the cord would take a quarter of an hour to reach the galley. In that time the galley would have become filled with an explosive mixture of gas and air. And by then he'd have reached the yacht club overlooking the Backwaters, and be gazing out

111

of the window when she blew up.

No trace of his handiwork would survive, and the explosion would be taken as another boating accident due to carelessness with bottled gas. With a glance at his watch, the man jumped into the dinghy, started the outboard and sped away into the mist.

Fifteen minutes later, exactly on time, a bright orange ball of fire erupted into the night sky. It was followed a second later by a blast of sound that rattled the windows of the yacht club and brought the dancers out onto the veranda.

Twelve

At eleven o'clock that night the yard foreman, Steve Gumbrell, phoned Fenella Forman and told her of her husband's accident.

Following the explosion, a flotilla of boats had set out across Horsey Mere heading for the blazing wreckage in Hamford Water. The Inshore Rescue boat on station in Walton Channel was first on the scene, her searchlights illuminating the whole area. The crew directed the fire hose at the burning yacht and sprayed it with foam, quickly extinguishing the fire. As the searchlights played on the smouldering hulk it became evident that the explosion had torn out the deck and the entire mid-section of the yacht.

On the way there, the coxswain had received a radio message that Robert Forman was on the yacht and, manoeuvring alongside, he put a crewman aboard to investigate. When the crewman gave the thumbs-down sign the rescue team turned the searchlights on the surrounding water and began scanning the floating debris for his body.

By now a number of other boats had reached the scene including the police launch, *Alert III*, from Harwich. The police sergeant took command and organised a wider search. But it was difficult to coordinate operations in the dark and after two hours the search was called off until daybreak.

"You'd best prepare yourself for the worst, Mrs Forman," Steve Gumbrell told Fenella on the phone. "There's not much hope of him being alive."

"Poor Bobby," she said. "What a dreadful thing to happen to him."

Millson learned of the accident when his daughter arrived home earlier than expected.

"The disco fizzled out because a boat blew up on the Backwaters and half the people left to help," she told him.

"What boat was it?"

"They said it was the *Lady Madonna*."

Millson frowned. "Anyone hurt?"

"Yes, someone was killed. They were searching for his body."

"Whose?"

"Jackie's father said it was Bobby Forman. He was a friend of his, apparently. Anyway, he let us wait on his boat in the deepwater pool until he was ready to take us home. It's a *lovely* boat." Dena went into raptures over Gordon Delayney's yacht and its state-of-the-art fittings. "It has a television … fridge … a shower … and an electric loo!" she said, wide-eyed.

Millson wondered if he should phone Helen, and decided to leave it until morning. She might not have been told yet, and it was better for someone in the family to be the first to break the news of her brother's death.

He gave Scobie a ring instead and told him what had

happened. "We'd better bring Monday's visit forward to tomorrow," he said, "and we'll have to make do with questioning Gumbrell instead of Forman."

There was a police car in attendance when Millson and Scobie arrived at the boatyard next morning. A bundle wrapped in a black plastic bag was being transferred from a launch to a waiting van.

On the quay, a woman stood with Steve Gumbrell, silently watching. Millson recognised Fenella Forman from Helen's description of her sister-in-law as a 'Cleopatra look-alike'.

A constable approached Millson and saluted. "That's the torso, sir. They found it half an hour ago. It floated out on the tide and ended up on Skipper's Island. They're still looking for the arms and legs."

"Keep your voice down, Constable," Millson muttered. "The widow's standing over there. Does anyone know what caused the explosion?"

"The fire team say it was a gas leak."

Millson nodded and walked across the quay to Fenella Forman. "I'm very sorry about your husband, Mrs Forman," he said.

"Thank you." She was white-faced, but composed.

Millson looked at Gumbrell and jerked his head in the direction of the yard's office. "We'd like a word, Mr Gumbrell."

"Yeah, OK." Walking towards the shed he asked, "What d'you want with me?"

"Didn't Mr Forman tell you we'd be coming to ask more questions?"

"No, never said anything to me."

"Well, you'll have to answer them now," Millson said, stepping into the shed and making for the office at the far end. "And for a start we'd like to take another look at that booking ledger."

"Help yourself," Gumbrell said. "It's there on his desk. I don't have anything to do with the hiring. Guv'nor did all that."

"D'you have any other Moody 38s on your books?"

"Yeah, three. They're all there in the book."

As Scobie stepped forward and began examining the entries, Millson asked, "What was Mr Forman doing out there on the *Lady Madonna* last night?"

"Testing the engine. She's had a new pump fitted and the guy that owns her wanted to use her this weekend."

"Would that be Greg Henderson?"

"Yeah, that's him."

Scobie straightened up from writing in his notebook. "I've taken the names and addresses of the people who had a Moody 38 on charter on the twenty-first of June." He turned to Gumbrell. "Can they take these boats across the Channel?"

"Sure. As long as the guv'nor's satisfied the skipper's got the know-how and experience."

"What d'you reckon to suicide, Norris?" Millson asked as he drove away.

"*Suicide?*" Scobie stared at him. "Why suicide?"

"Perhaps to avoid prison and bringing shame on his family."

"But he hasn't done anything wrong, as far as we know. And, anyway, no one would choose to kill himself that way," Scobie said.

"He might if he wanted his death to look like an accident. An inquest would dig into the reasons for a suicide, and then whatever he'd done would come out."

Scobie shook his head. "I don't buy any of it."

"Neither do I," Millson said cheerfully. "I was just trying it on you for size."

At lunch-time Helen Forman phoned Millson to thank him for the message of condolence he'd left on her answerphone earlier that morning.

"Would you come to the funeral?" she asked. "It's on Wednesday."

"That's pretty quick, isn't it?"

"Fenella never wasted much time where Bobby was concerned." Her tone was acid. "Quick engagement ... quick marriage ... and now a quick funeral." She sounded bitter.

"Yes, of course I'll come." He'd intended going anyway.

After the call he went next door to Scobie's room. "D'you possess a black tie, Norris?"

"Yes."

"Good. Then you can come to Bobby Forman's funeral with me."

"Any particular reason?"

"Yes, to keep me company," Millson said. "Emotional affairs, funerals. You never know what might happen."

The post-mortem later that day was carried out by a local doctor on the coroner's list of suitably qualified doctors. He had only the torso to work on, but soon concluded Robert Forman's death was caused by the blast of a gas explosion. At the inquest on Monday, attended only by Fenella and a lone journalist, the coroner recorded a verdict of death by misadventure.

For the benefit of the reporter he added the comment that in his district, with its coastal boundaries, boating accidents with bottled gas were an all too frequent occurrence and people should take more care.

Robert Forman was buried beside his mother in the family grave at Christ Church in Coggeshall. At the end of the service in the church Millson and Scobie followed the cortège to the open grave for the committal service.

The vicar conducted the burial ceremony from the head of the grave and Fenella Forman, dressed in black, stood alone at the foot. Ruth and her husband were on one side of the grave, and a bewildered-looking Edward Forman on the other, flanked either side by Helen and his wife, Christine. Millson and Scobie stood with the other mourners in the background.

When the coffin had been lowered into the ground, and the service concluded, Fenella stooped and gathered a handful of soil for the final ritual. As she sprinkled it on the coffin, there was a sudden shout.

"Whore!" The single word reverberated through the circle of mourners like a thunderclap.

Eddie Forman was straining forward, his eyes wild, as his wife and daughter struggled to hold him back. Into the shocked silence he snarled, "Harlot! Adulteress!" Stretching his neck forward like a turtle, he spat at Fenella.

Hushing him, Helen and Christine Forman dragged him away to the rear of the gathering. Quentin Page pulled out a handkerchief and, stepping over to Fenella, wiped the spittle from her shocked face.

Millson turned to Scobie. "There now ... what did I tell you?"

"Come on, you didn't *know* this was going to happen," Scobie said. "You were just—" He broke off as Helen Forman came towards them.

"Thank you for coming," she said. Her eyes were wet with tears. "I'm sorry about Dad. I can't imagine why he attacked Fenella like that. Would you like to come to the house? You're very welcome."

"Thank you, but we have to get back," Millson said.

"Oh ... right. Um ..." She hesitated. "You know I told you Dad never visited Piers and Mary? Well, he did. It was meant to be a reconciliation but when he discovered Piers couldn't give Mary children, it just made him more bitter. I didn't tell you because I didn't want you bothering him, and he really doesn't remember anything about them." She turned on her heel and walked quickly away.

Millson gazed after her as she rejoined her father and Christine. "That's one of the peculiarities about funerals, Norris. People like to clear their consciences. The other peculiarity, of course, is that funerals of murder victims are often attended by their killer." He began walking towards the gate. "What d'you make of Eddie Forman's outburst?"

"I don't think he's as vague as they think. He was very definite about Fenella."

"He certainly was," Millson agreed. "And we can't ignore an accusation like that. Not considering the way her husband met his death. We'll give Christine Forman a call tomorrow and ask her what Eddie meant by it."

Christine Forman was still wearing mourning clothes when Millson and Scobie called next day. Her blonde hair was uncombed and her eyes were red and puffy from crying. Eddie was on his weekly outing with Social Services she informed them as she led them into the small sitting-room off the hall.

"My little hideaway," she said, stooping quickly to pick up a framed photograph lying on the floor by an armchair. She sat down in the chair, keeping the photograph face down on her lap. Millson wondered why she was holding a portrait of Bobby Forman.

"I'm sorry to trouble you at a time like this, Mrs Forman," he said as they seated themselves, "but I'm hoping you can enlighten us on your husband's outburst at the funeral yesterday."

"Oh, you mustn't mind Eddie, Chief Inspector. He often says strange things. He even said he saw one of his brother's foster sons at the funeral. Nonsense, of course. How could he possibly recognise him?"

"Well, he did visit them once. Helen told us yesterday," Millson said.

"Yes, I know. She told me too. But that was twenty years ago. Eddie wouldn't know him now."

Millson nodded agreement. "He was very emphatic about the other thing he said, though. He called his daughter-in-law an adulteress. Is it true?"

His bluntness startled her. "I – um ..." She seemed confused. "Does it matter?"

"I'm afraid it does. When a husband has an unusual fatal accident, and an accusation like that is made against his wife, it has to be looked into."

"I see." She looked down at her hands. "I thought Bobby had only told me. But he must have told his father too." She raised her head and looked at Millson. "Yes, Fenella was being unfaithful. Bobby was sure of it."

"Who with?"

Again his directness alarmed her. "A man called Gregory Henderson." She saw Millson's face change. "Do you know him?"

"Sergeant Scobie does."

"It was his yacht Bobby was—" She stopped, her eyes wide. "Oh my God! You don't think—?" She stopped again. "It *was* an accident, wasn't it?"

"That was the coroner's verdict," Millson said.

"I don't know where the man lives," she went on, "but I expect the boatyard will have his address."

"Thank you, we already know it," Millson said. "Did your stepson confide anything else to you?"

He was surprised to see her blush like a young girl. "Only personal things, Chief Inspector – about his marriage and so on. He's always brought his troubles to me. His mother died when he was quite young, you see."

Millson nodded and rose to his feet. "Well, thank you for your time, Mrs Forman. We shan't trouble you any further."

"You will let me know if …" She hesitated. "If there was anything wrong about Bobby's death? I know I was only his stepmother, but I have a right to know."

"Yes, of course," Millson said.

"Tell me about Henderson, Norris," Millson said as he drove away.

"Good-looking … swish flat in the City, which he says goes with the job."

"What job?"

"He works for a finance company. Calls himself a market trader. I think he had money problems, though, because he told me he couldn't keep up the payments on the *Lady Madonna*, and that's why he made the deal with Forman."

"Right. Let's see what the boatyard know about him, then."

Christine Forman heard their car drive away and slumped down in her chair. She wished she could just lie there and die. Her life had no purpose any more. It was meaningless without Bobby to give her a future to look forward to when Eddie died. Now there was only the endless drudge of looking after him, and she didn't think she could bear it much longer.

"Oh, Bobby ... dearest Bobby." She began to cry.

She lifted his picture and held it to her breast, pressing it hard against her nipples and rubbing it back and forth until the pain brought a sobbing release.

Thirteen

Steve Gumbrell and another man were gathering up rubbish and old timbers and piling them on a large bonfire when Millson and Scobie drove into the yard at Kirby-le-Soken.

"What d'you lot want?" Gumbrell scowled at them as they picked their way through the debris and came towards him.

"Information," Scobie said. "What's going on?"

Gumbrell heaved a king-size baulk of timber on to the burning pile. "She turns up here eight o'clock this morning giving out orders to me and Aubrey," he said angrily. "Says she owns the yard now. Tells us the place looks like a tip and we're to get it cleared up at once. She wants to rearrange the layout and have the whole place repainted. Women!" He wiped his hands on his overalls. "What d'you want to know?"

"Tell us about your late boss and his wife." Millson coughed as a puff of wind billowed smoke in his face. "Let's move further away."

"Yeah, OK. Over here," Gumbrell led them upwind of

the fire to some old galvanised water tanks that had been used to support the smaller boats. "Least she knows what she's doing," he said grudgingly, as he sat down and surveyed the partially cleared yard. "Which is more'n he did."

"Mr Forman no good at the business, then?" Scobie asked.

Gumbrell made a face. "Knew about boats ... didn't know his arse from his elbow when it came to running a boatyard, though. He'd been a bank manager, see?"

"So, how did he come to own a boatyard?"

"Lost his job when they chopped the staff. He got a big dollop of redundancy money and decides to start a yacht chartering business. Comes down here looking for a yard to buy and Bill Symes – my old guv'nor, who used to own the place – spins him a yarn about prospects and that, and sells out to him quick. Laughs his head off in the Ship every night about it, Bill does."

"What about Mrs Forman," Millson asked.

"Ah, now she's a sharp one, she is. Use to live here in Kirby before she married. Right little goer too, she was. A lot of raised eyebrows when people heard she'd hooked a bank manager. But he didn't come from round here, so he didn't know what she was like. Not that she ain't a good looker, and with a good job in the City and that."

"Tell me about Gregory Henderson."

"He owns the *Lady M* – or what's left of her."

"I know that. What's his relationship with Mrs Forman?"

Gumbrell smirked. "They's pretty chummy, I guess."

"Meaning?"

"I was at the meeting back in April when her and the guv'nor was trying to do the deal for the *Lady M* with

Henderson. He was giving it the thumbs down. So she gives him the come-on with her eyes." Gumbrell leered. "Never seen the like of that look. 'You can have me if you sign the contract,' it said. Clear as if she'd said it out loud." He gave a throaty chuckle. "Next thing you know, he was signing. Take it from me, it was her got the *Lady Madonna* for us. And I reckon she's been keeping Henderson happy ever since, 'cos this morning she tells me she's making him a partner."

"A partner in the business?"

"Yep. Speaks for itself, don't it?"

The man feeding the bonfire threw an open can of paint on it and a tongue of flame shot into the air. The sudden burst of fire triggered a thought in Millson's mind.

"Last time we were here you told us Mr Forman was working on the boat because Henderson wanted it for the weekend. When did Henderson tell him that?" he asked.

"He phoned Friday afternoon. Said he wanted her ready for next day."

"So he would have known Mr Forman was out there working on it that evening?"

"Yeah, course."

They interviewed Gregory Henderson at his flat in the Barbican in the evening. Scobie had made the appointment for eight o'clock, but Millson decided to arrive half an hour early. "To put him on edge," he told Scobie.

Henderson seemed relaxed, however, as he offered them drinks. When they declined he poured himself one.

"I don't understand why you've come to see me," he said. "Bobby's death was an accident and the coroner returned a verdict of misadventure."

"Something has come up, and we think you may be able to help us, Mr Henderson," Millson said in a friendly tone, lowering himself into one of the armchairs. The soft leather embraced his frame so comfortably he thought it must be air-filled. "My sergeant and I don't know anything about boats," he said, with a warning glance at Scobie. "We're hoping you can give us an idea of how the accident happened."

Henderson remained standing, his eyes suspicious. "The fire service said there was a leak of butane gas, and an accidental spark must have caused an explosion. Why on earth should you think I know any more than they do?"

"Because it was your yacht, Mr Henderson. And you – knowing the layout, any little faults there might be – would know better than the firemen what might have happened."

"Well, I don't," Henderson said curtly.

"You see, what bothers me," Millson went on, as though Henderson hadn't spoken, "is that Mr Forman was an experienced yachtsman like yourself. He was, wasn't he?"

"I believe so."

"And he'd know all about the dangers of bottled gas, wouldn't he?"

"Yes, I imagine so."

"So, how could he make such a silly mistake?"

"I don't know, and I don't understand why you're asking *me* these questions, Chief Inspector."

"Because you and his wife are lovers, that's why," Millson said.

Henderson flinched. "I see," he said, his mouth tightening. He moved to a tubular steel chair and sat down. "So *this* is what it's about. The post-mortem and coroner's inquest aren't good enough for you, and you're poking into people's private lives to see what dirt you can find. Well, you're wasting your time. Robert's death was an accident, and it was nothing to do with Fenella and me."

"On good terms with him, were you?"

"It was a business relationship. I loaned him the *Lady Madonna*, and his yard maintained her and let her out on charter for six months of the year. I received a percentage of the income, and had use of her for the other six months."

"Did he know of your relationship with his wife?"

"No, of course not."

"Are you sure?"

"Fenella was certain he didn't."

"Uh-huh. So, what's the situation between you two now?"

"We're planning to get married ... after a decent interval. Not that it's any of your business."

"Very convenient, then, his accident," Millson said. "Removes a barrier, so to speak."

"I resent the implication," Henderson said angrily. "I didn't kill Bobby. Why should I?"

"Because you wanted his wife – and she wanted the business. I hear she's making you a partner."

"I'm sick of this!" Henderson said angrily. "The man's death was an accident, and everyone except you accepts that."

Unperturbed, Millson wriggled free of the embracing leather and sat forward. "Where were you last Friday evening when the accident happened?"

"I was here ... in this flat."

"Anyone to verify that?"

Scobie had taken out his notebook. Henderson stared at

Scobie's poised pen. "No."

"Did you go out at all?"

"No."

"I understand you phoned Mr Forman late that afternoon and told him you wanted *Lady Madonna* ready to take out the next day."

For the first time Henderson hesitated. "That's right."

"What did he say?"

"He said OK, the engineer was away, but he'd check the engine for me himself."

"So you knew he'd be out there on the water alone that evening."

"Yes, I suppose so. I didn't think about it."

Millson lay back in the chair again and nodded at Scobie.

Scobie said, "When I was here before, Mr Henderson, I asked you where the *Lady Madonna* was the night a man's body was found on Dengie. The twenty-first of June. You remember?"

"Of course."

"Can I ask the same question about you?"

"You mean, where was *I*? How extraordinary. I've no idea. I'll look in my diary." He took a pocket diary from inside his jacket and turned the pages. "I was here, in the flat."

"Anyone to confirm that?"

"No." Henderson's tone was hostile.

"Why did you want the yacht last weekend? What were you planning to do?"

"I was going to sail her to Harwich and up the Stour to Mistley."

Scobie raised his eyebrows. "Mistley? That's close by

Manningtree, where the Formans live," he said.

"That's right." Henderson shrugged. "If you must know, Fenella was planning to slip away and join me for a while."

"Very convenient," Scobie said.

"Yes." Henderson glared at him. "So, it would have been very *inconvenient* – and stupid – to blow up the yacht the night before, wouldn't it?"

Millson stirred in his seat. "That could just be a cover story," he said.

"I've had enough of this!" Henderson stood up. "It's quite obvious you have no evidence to connect me with Bobby Forman's death. Yes, I admit I was having an affair with his wife. But I'm not putting up with this line of questioning if that's all you have against me."

"Very well." Millson struggled out of the clinging armchair. "We'll continue our inquiries. In the meantime, I expect you to be available for further questions if we need you."

At the door he paused. "Were you at the funeral, Mr Henderson?"

"Yes, to give Fenella support. I didn't attend the service, though. That would have upset the family."

"He seemed pretty confident," Scobie said as they drove along London Wall. "Perhaps it *was* an accident."

"When a man is killed just before we're due to question him about a suspected murder, and his wife is having an affair, I need a lot of convincing his death was an accident," Millson said. "Let's see how the grieving widow makes out tomorrow."

Fourteen

The next morning Millson had a phone call from the Leeds police. They had located Sandra Mitchell. Or rather they had found the address where she'd been living until two months ago. She'd left there in a hurry two weeks after the body was discovered at Great Yeldham.

"That means she knows something," Millson told his colleague in Leeds.

"Or maybe she just doesn't want to be involved. Toms don't like answering questions and helping the police."

"No, that's not why she did a runner," Millson said. "There had been no mention of foster children, or an appeal for her then. The reason she took off was because she knows about the murder. We must find her. She's the only real lead we have."

"OK. We'll dig out any friends or associates she had. Maybe one of them will know where she went."

"Thanks." Millson put down the phone. He was puzzled why Sandra Mitchell had run off so soon after the body was found. It was long before she could have thought the police might question her. What had she been afraid of?

He pulled a notepad towards him and began to draft a carefully worded appeal. In it he said the police believed Sandra Mitchell, who was known to have been living at an address in Leeds until two months ago, held vital information in connection with a murder and it was imperative she contacted them urgently. He indicated that the police were not concerned with any misdeeds she might have committed herself. They were only interested in information about the murder, and would protect her if she had any fears for her safety. Hoping this reassurance would persuade her to come forward, he sent the draft to the press officer for release.

It depressed him that Sandra was his only lead. There had still been no response from the two other foster children, Barry Naylor and Alan Stigall, nor to his appeal for Sean Kebble. And what depressed him further was that no one, apart from Sean's mother, had offered any information about them.

The only scrap he had was about Barry Naylor. The team patiently sifting the missing persons reports for twenty years ago had come across one for Barry. He'd been reported missing a year after he absconded from the Formans. The report had been sent in by the warden of the hostel in Wickford where Barry was then living. The hostel had been closed long ago, but the team had traced one of the staff who worked there.

"We've spoken to him," a WDC told Millson. "He remembers Barry at the Wickford hostel with Sean Kebble. He says Barry was going after a holiday job in Cromer and promised to let them know how he got on. He was still only sixteen, and when they didn't hear from him again they reported him missing."

Had Barry disappeared because he'd committed murder? Or was he dead? Millson wondered. Sandra Mitchell might know, if only he could find her. She and Barry had been together at the Formans' when they lived in Wickford.

When Millson and Scobie went to interview Fenella Forman that evening, a red Toyota MR2 was parked in the drive of the house in Manningtree.

"Spending hubby's money already by the look of it," Scobie said sourly.

"Now, now, Norris," said Millson. "Let's keep an open mind, shall we?"

The Fenella who opened the door to them was very different to the pale-faced woman in black who'd stood on the quay and watched her husband's torso being brought ashore. Her cheeks were a glowing pink, her glossy black hair had been recently coiffured, and she was wearing bright red slacks with a long-tailed white shirt over them.

There were several large cardboard boxes in the hallway, some lying open and half-packed.

"Moving, Mrs Forman?" Millson asked.

"No. I'm packing all Bobby's things to send over to Coggeshall. I don't want them. The family can sort them out." She had a distinctive, deep-toned voice. Millson, who before then had only heard her say a faint 'thank you' at the boatyard, was struck by its resonance and power.

She led them into a front room. Around a low, glass-topped table were three swivel chairs on short pedestals, similar to dentists' chairs. Dropping neatly into one, she signalled Millson and Scobie to sit in the other two.

Scobie did so without difficulty, but Millson's weight, as he sat down, tilted the chair backwards towards the horizontal. He quickly threw his weight forward and the chair came suddenly upright, almost tipping him out.

Politely ignoring his antics, Fenella said, "Greg phoned me, so I know why you're here, Chief Inspector. This is all because that old fool shot his mouth off at the funeral."

"We do have to consider the implications in a case like this, Mrs Forman," Millson said, having achieved a satisfactory angle with his chair.

"By 'in a case like this', you mean where a husband has a fatal accident, and the wife has a lover?" Her tone was waspish.

"Exactly," Millson said, smiling pleasantly. "An unusual accident too. So, you won't mind answering a few questions, I hope."

"Anything to clear your mind, Chief Inspector." She returned his smile with one of her own. "I hope it's a nice clean mind."

"More importantly, it's an open mind, Mrs Forman."

"It didn't seem so to Mr Henderson," she said, her voice suddenly hard.

Millson ignored the criticism. "I gather you met Mr Henderson earlier this year?"

"Yes, in April, when he brought the *Lady Madonna* to us for charter." She smiled again, a mocking smile this time. "But you already know that, don't you? And a lot more." Her eyes flashed. "I made Gumbrell repeat everything he said to you – exactly as he said it."

Scobie saw her eyes flare and had a vision of Fenella Forman striding towards Gumbrell flourishing a whip.

Greg had phoned Fenella immediately the police left the night before, and she'd driven to the yard first thing that morning.

Aubrey Smith heard the crunch of tyres on shingle and looked up from scrubbing the underside of a motor-cruiser. Fenella Forman's red Toyota sports car was turning into the yard.

He called to Steve Gumbrell, who was sitting on an upturned dinghy smoking a cigarette. "Boss Lady's here, Steve."

Steve Gumbrell stood up, and stamped out his cigarette. Grabbing one of Aubrey's scrubbing brushes, he pretended to be scrubbing the dinghy he'd been sitting on.

Fenella stepped out of her car and looked in his direction. She was not holding the whip Scobie had visualised, she was holding a mobile phone and she stabbed it at Steve Gumbrell like a weapon.

"You!" She pointed the phone at the shed where her new office was being built. "In there. Now!" She strode towards the shed.

Underneath the motor-cruiser, Aubrey sniggered. "She don't sound very happy, Steve."

"Bossy bitch! Who does she think she is?" Gumbrell threw down the scrubbing-brush and marched after her.

Inside the shed she rounded on him furiously. "I want to know exactly what you've told the police about me. Word for word."

As he opened his mouth to protest she said venomously, "Don't argue with me. I know enough about you and your pilfering to put you in prison. Now get on with it!"

"I told him I'd sack him if he didn't," Fenella told Millson. "I don't employ people who don't obey me."

"I see." Millson was irritated she'd pre-empted his questions. Before he could rearrange them she went on:

"Let me tell you something, Chief Inspector. My marriage

was a total failure because my husband had hang-ups about his stepmother that went right back to adolescence. He was obsessed with her. I don't know if he actually went to bed with her, but he certainly did in his mind."

"If the marriage was such a failure, why didn't you leave him and get a divorce?" he asked.

"Money. Greg has no capital worth speaking of, and neither do I. Also, his job isn't secure, and I didn't fancy love in a bedsit if he lost it," she said calmly.

"Whereas now you have the business, and you've made him your business partner."

"That's right. I wasted five years of my life with Bobby. Now I want to get on with it … fast."

Scobie looked up from his notebook and asked in a shocked voice, "Don't you have any regrets over your husband's death, Mrs Forman?"

She turned her large eyes on him. "No, I don't. Why should I? I didn't love him. And he certainly didn't love me. All he wanted was to get into Christine's knickers. Though I don't think she let him – not the way he still wanted sex with me." Her eyes stared boldly into Scobie's until he dropped his in embarrassment.

Millson said, "So you and your lover were glad to be rid of him."

"Yes." She practically spat the word out. "But we had nothing to do with his accident." She looked straight at him, her gaze steady and unblinking.

Millson was silent for a while. Fenella Forman was cool and controlled. And very, very determined. He hadn't the slightest doubt she was capable of murder and would carry it out with ruthless efficiency. If she and Henderson had planned the accident, and murdered her husband, he wanted very strong evidence before he'd risk confronting her with it. At the moment he had nothing.

He manoeuvred himself carefully from his seat and stood up. "Well, thank you, Mrs Forman. We'll let you get on with your packing."

Her expression didn't alter but he detected tell-tale signs of relief – a slight relaxation in the shoulders, a slackening of tension around the mouth. Fenella Forman was relieved they were leaving. Was it guilt? Or simply natural tension over an interview by the police?

At the front door as they left she smiled at Scobie with eyes that were now soft and luminous. Scobie felt the flow of their caressing warmth like the touch of fingers stroking his face.

"That woman could turn a man on just by looking at him," he said in an aggrieved tone as they drove away.

Millson grinned. "Real come-to-bed eyes, weren't they? And that remarkable voice."

"Sounded like a foghorn to me," Scobie said. "She's a woman who gets what she wants and tramples on anyone in her way. She wanted the business and loverboy wanted her. So they killed the poor sod because he was in the way."

"All right, tell me how they faked the accident, then."

"OK." Scobie stretched his long legs further into the passenger well. "Henderson knew Forman would be working alone on the *Lady Madonna* that night. So he drove down there from London, snitched a dinghy and went out to the yacht. There was a heavy mist so he wasn't seen. He boarded the yacht and killed Forman – probably strangled him because that would escape detection after he'd been blown to bits."

"How did he manage to blow up the boat without blowing himself up too?"

"He used some means of delaying the ignition. A candle left burning in a jam jar would do. He set up a slow gas leak – loosening a connection, or turning a tap on slightly. Nothing would happen until the mix of air and gas reached flashpoint. At that point the candle flame would detonate it. By which time he was well away."

Millson nodded. "That's ingenious, Norris. I like it."

Scobie said cautiously, "It's only a theory, mind. I've never heard of a murder being committed like that." He waited for Millson to cite a similar case, as usual.

But Millson said, "Neither have I. The problem is we don't have a shred of evidence to show Henderson did any such thing."

He drove for a while in silence, his thoughts straying from Robert Forman's accident to last night's scene with his daughter. She'd been to a party at Jacqueline Delayney's house. It had been organised by Jackie's father as compensation for the failure of the yacht club disco.

Dena came home around midnight, her cheeks flushed and a scarf round her neck.

"Something the matter with your throat?" he asked, as she made for the stairs.

"No."

"So, are you going to wear that scarf in bed?"

"Oh ... I forgot." She turned back, hung the scarf on a peg in the hall, and made for the stairs again.

"Just a minute, young lady. What are those marks on your neck?"

"It's nothing. We played Murder and the guy who pretended to strangle me overdid it a bit."

He stepped closer and peered at the red weals. "They're love bites," he said.

"They're not!" Her voice was shrill. Which meant they were, but he let it go and she turned and bolted up the stairs.

"Most of the people at the party were much older than her, Norris. She's too young for that sort of thing," Millson said as he told Scobie about the incident.

"I shouldn't take it seriously, George. I had a girlfriend of nine when I was a lad. I loved her passionately, and we were going to run away and get married."

"That's kids' stuff! This isn't the same thing at all."

"She was only necking," Scobie said.

"Yes, and then comes petting, and next thing I know she'll be wanting to go on the Pill."

"At *thirteen*? I don't think so, George. Dena's not like that. Anyway, weren't the parents around?"

Millson snorted. "Only Jackie's father, and I wouldn't put much faith in him. He's an actor and he's hardly ever there. He's always swanning off to some film location or other and leaving the girls on their own."

"Actor? What's his name?"

"Gordon Delayney."

"Never heard of him."

"Well, he must earn good money. According to Dena he owns a luxury yacht that is out of this world."

"Really? I wonder where—" Scobie stopped and shot upright in his seat. "Hell!" he said.

Millson glanced at him. "What's bitten you?"

"What kind of yacht?"

"*I* don't know," Millson said. "Why?"

"There was a Gordon Delayney on the fax from Swansea. But the address was in Majorca and I assumed that's where the yacht was kept. It was a Westerly Overlord. It has to be the one we're looking for. Where does he live?"

"In Wivenhoe," Millson said. "But before you go rushing in, just remember the only connection between the yacht and the body on Dengie is she was seen there the same night."

"Yes, OK. I'll give him a ring."

"Better if I don't come," Millson said. "Dena's close friends with his younger daughter. There's a couple of questions you can ask him for me, though. His daughter told me the grandparents have a cottage at Great Yeldham and her father used to spend time there as a boy. Ask him about that. And ask if he went to Bobby Forman's funeral."

"Is this to do with your theory about murderers attending their victims' funerals?"

"Not theory. Fact. Just ask, Norris. Don't try to read my mind."

Scobie put his head round Millson's door next morning and said, "Delayney flew to Italy early this morning. I've spoken to his agent in London and it seems he won't be back for a week. So I'm seeing his daughter Jacqueline after school today. She might be able to help."

"Take a woman police officer with you, Norris. Jackie Delayney is jailbait."

Scobie laughed. "That's just your paternal prejudice showing, George."

Scobie arrived at Gordon Delayney's house on the waterfront at Wivenhoe at six o'clock. When Jackie Delayney opened the door and led him to the sitting-room overlooking the river, he saw the reason for George

Millson's comment. Her white school blouse bulged in a way that suggested it was time she began wearing a bra, and the minuscule black skirt scarcely covered her bottom.

She sat him down in a low armchair and sat in one opposite, somehow managing to sit decorously, not showing her knickers. "You're the one Dena calls Copperknob," she said, grinning at him. "Would you like a drink?"

He realised she didn't mean tea or coffee. "Er – no, thank you."

"I told George about Granddad's cottage in Great Yeldham ages ago. It's taken him a long time to catch on." She saw his raised eyebrows. "That *is* what you've come about, isn't it?"

"Not really. It's your father's yacht, *Seaspray*, I'm interested in."

"Oh." She sounded disappointed. "What about it?"

"We'd like to establish where she was one night in June."

"How should I know?" she said crossly. "Have you tried asking him?"

Scobie kept his temper and said calmly, "Your father's in Italy – as I'm sure you know – and he won't be back for a week. So, I came here hoping you could help me. Now, if you can't help, perhaps I should speak to your sister." He stood up.

"Oh no, don't go." Her mood suddenly changed. "What date in June?"

"The twenty-first."

"I'll have a look in his boat diary. There might be something there." She jumped up and went out of the room.

She returned moments later holding a small notebook. "He went to Boulogne and back the week before, but there's nothing down for the week beginning twenty-first of June. Nothing at all."

"I see. Does he often sail across the Channel?"

"Not that often. He doesn't get the time."

"Does he ever take you?"

"Sometimes in the hols. But usually he takes his latest squeeze." She smirked. "He's *very* good-looking. That's him." She pointed to a picture hanging on the wall.

Scobie looked at the studio portrait of Gordon Delayney posing as a Roman emperor. He had wavy blond hair, a lock of it falling over his forehead, wide blue eyes and lips that were full and sensuous. The muscles on his bare arms stood out like a boxer's and Scobie could well imagine many women tingling with pleasure at the prospect of being bedded by Gordon Delayney.

Jackie dropped the notebook on the sofa and sat down again. "What else would you like to know, Norris?" She lolled back in the armchair and crossed her legs, still managing to keep her crotch covered.

"This cottage your granddad had in Great Yeldham. I gather your dad spent school holidays there when he was a boy. When would that have been?"

"Well, he's thirty-nine now. You work it out."

Scobie calculated Delayney would have been seventeen when the murder was believed to have been committed and, allowing a year or so leeway, might have been in Great Yeldham at the time.

She was ahead of him. "So he could have done it, couldn't he?" she said, rounding her eyes dramatically.

"You want us to put your dad on our suspect list, then?" he asked jokingly.

"Ooh yes, he'd love that. Get him loads of publicity."

He smiled indulgently. "Your father was friends with Bobby Forman, I believe, Jackie. Did they go sailing together?"

"Oh no, it was more a business relationship. Dad uses the yard's moorings in Hamford Water, and they do the maintenance on *Seaspray*. You could ask them where she was that week in June."

"Yes, thank you. I will. Did your father go to Bobby's funeral?"

She sat up, looking alert, and he realised he should have been less obvious. "Yes, he did. Why?"

"Just proves he killed Bobby Forman too," he said, forcing a broad grin. "Don't you know the murderer always goes to his victim's funeral?"

"Ha-ha," she said coldly. "Very funny."

Fifteen

Scobie recounted Jacqueline Delayney's information to Millson next morning.

"Gordon Delayney was school age when the Yeldham murder was committed so he could have been on holiday there at the time. And, yes, he did go to Bobby Forman's funeral," Scobie said. "But we're no nearer knowing where his yacht was the night the body was found on Dengie. Except that according to his boat diary, she'd been on a trip to Boulogne the week before. His daughter told me her father had one of Forman's moorings on the Backwaters so it's worth asking Steve Gumbrell if he knows anything about *Seaspray*."

Millson nodded. "What did you think of the precocious Jackie, Norris?"

"She's not that bad. She's just a typical adolescent girl."

"Not to me, she isn't. She's a little minx."

"It's a phase girls go through. My kid sister was just like that."

"You mean Dena will be like that? Not if I have anything to do with it, she won't."

145

"I think you might have a problem there, George."

Millson grunted. "Let's go see Gumbrell before you depress me any more."

They found Steve Gumbrell in one of the sheds drinking tea with Aubrey Smith when they arrived at the yard.

"What is it now?" he demanded. "I got a lot of grief from the Boss Lady over what I said last time."

"Twisted your goolies till you squeaked, was the way she told it," Millson said cheerfully.

"This is not about Mrs Forman," Scobie said. "It's about a yacht called *Seaspray* owned by Gordon Delayney. We understand Mr Delayney sometimes puts his boat on your moorings here."

"That's right."

"Can you tell us if she was here on the twenty-first of June last?"

Gumbrell raised his eyebrows. "You still after that yacht at Dengie?"

"Yes. And we're fairly sure now it was his."

"I'll have to look in the office."

They followed him across the yard to the shed by the entrance gate. Inside, a carpenter was erecting partitioning.

"Boss Lady's having herself a proper office with a separate door," Gumbrell explained. He consulted a large scale chart of the Backwaters pinned to the wall. "Delayney has buoy number five." He flicked open a diary on the shelf below. "We keep a note of whether moorings are in use or not so we can let visitors use them." He ran his finger down a page. "Nope. *Seaspray* weren't here that week."

"And just for the record, Mr Gumbrell," Millson asked, "where were you that night?"

"Twenty-first of June?" Gumbrell wrinkled his forehead. "Don't rightly know that far back. Have to look in another book. All books, this place. Have to record my time, see?" He rummaged among the notebooks on the shelf, picked one out, and thumbed through it. He opened a page. "It was me afternoon off. Me and Aubrey went fishing. We took out *Arkle* and were off the Naze that night. Plenty of mackerel around there."

"Was that Aubrey you were drinking tea with?"

"Yeah, that's him. Want me to call him?" Gumbrell reached for the intercom handset.

"No." Millson nodded to Scobie. "Go and have a word with him, Sergeant."

As Scobie went out, Millson said casually, "What did you think of Mr Forman's accident?" He looked around for a chair. Finding none, he lifted himself onto a bench against the wall. "Bit unusual, wasn't it?"

"Boss Lady don't seem to think so." Gumbrell leered at him. "But then she wouldn't, would she?"

"You think she and Henderson rigged it?"

Gumbrell said quickly, "No. An' I'm not saying no more. 'Cos soon as she hears you've bin here she'll want a word by word report on what I said."

"Or she'll twist your balls again, eh?" Millson grinned.

"No, I'll be out of a job," Gumbrell muttered.

"All right. Let's stick with the facts. What time did Mr Forman go out to the *Lady Madonna* that evening?"

"About seven, I reckon."

"Was anyone else here then?"

"Only me."

"And when did you leave?"

"About an hour later. There was nothing doing, so I went off."

147

"Home?"

"No, I drove over to the yacht club for a drink."

"Was the yard locked?"

"Not that night, 'cos the guv'nor was still to come ashore. He told me he'd lock up when he'd finished."

"So, after you left, someone could have slipped in here, borrowed a dinghy, and gone out to the *Lady Madonna*?"

"I s'pose so."

"And where were you when the yacht exploded?"

"Up in the veranda bar of the club. I saw the flash as she went up. About nine o'clock, it was."

"Many other people in the bar?"

"Yeah, lots. There was a disco going on down below. Soon as I saw the direction of the blaze I had a feeling it might be the *Lady M*. I went off in the launch to help."

The door opened and Scobie re-entered. "Smith confirms his story," he said.

"Right then." Millson slid down from the bench. "That's all, Mr Gumbrell."

"Well, that didn't get us anywhere," Scobie said as he opened the car door. "We'll have to leave it until Delayney comes back now."

"You'd better tell his agent we want to speak to him, else he'll be gone again before you know it," Millson said. "And I want you to check something for me. Gumbrell said he was drinking in the yacht club bar the night Forman's boat blew up. You're a member. See if you can find anyone who saw him there and can tell you what time he arrived."

In the afternoon, Helen Forman phoned Millson from the hospital. "Dad's been rambling about the foster children again. Can we meet for a drink?"

"Red Lion at six?" he suggested.

"Yes, and it's my turn," she said.

Millson was already at the bar when Helen Forman entered. He watched her approaching, the uniform fitting her slim figure perfectly, and wondered why some women looked good in uniform while others looked like a sack of potatoes.

As he turned to the bar to order she said quickly, "It's my shout, remember?" She glanced at his half-empty glass. "What are you drinking?"

"I'll have a beer, please."

"Come on, that's not a beer glass," she said.

"All right, then. A whisky."

She turned to the waiting barman. "And I'll have the same," she said.

"You drink whisky?" Millson asked in surprise.

"Only when I'm upset. I saw Dad yesterday evening."

"How is he?"

"Much worse, I'm afraid. This dreadful Alzheimer's is wiping out his memory. Short-term memory goes first and most of the time now he only remembers when he was a young man. So he doesn't recognise us sometimes because he remembers us as children, not grown-ups. And last night …" She stopped, and looked away from him.

Eddie Forman had jerked his head away when his daughter kissed him.

"It's Helen, Dad."

He stared at her vacantly. "Where's your mother, Lena?" he asked querulously, using his pet name for her as a child.

Then his face came to life, and he turned frightened eyes

149

on her. "Hallo, Helen, love. Have you come to see your old Dad?" He smiled at her.

She wasn't quick enough and he caught her expression of horror. His smile died. "I was gone again, wasn't I?"

"Don't worry about it, Dad. I'm here."

He reached up and clutched her arm. "Listen! While I'm thinking straight," he said. "Soon I'll be dribbling like a baby … having to be fed … taken to the loo. I don't want that."

"It's not going to happen." But she knew it was.

He reached up and clutched her arm. "Don't let them put me away, Helen." His voice was strong now, and urgent. "I don't want to live like that. You're a nurse – you *know* what to do." When she didn't answer his voice rose. "Listen, girl! I know what I'm saying! Now promise me." His grip on her arm tightened painfully. "Promise!"

"All right! I promise." She fought back her tears and cradled his head against her breast. "It's all right," she said soothingly. "I understand. I understand."

He let out a long sigh and sank back in the chair. "You're a good girl, Helen. I know you won't let me down."

Millson was looking at her expectantly. "The terrible thing is, he *knows* what's happening to him. He asked me—" She broke off.

Millson reached out and touched her hand. "I'm so very sorry, Helen," he said. "I wish there were something helpful I could say."

"It helps just telling you about it," she said. "I can't talk to Ruth or Christine. It would be too painful."

She wanted to go on and tell him everything. He was a policeman, though, and you couldn't tell a policeman something like that. She took a mouthful of whisky. "And now my brother-in-law wants Dad put in a home. He's called a family meeting for tomorrow evening to discuss it." She drained her glass. "But I haven't brought you here to listen to my family problems. Last night Dad had one of his lucid periods and he told me about the man he saw at Bobby's funeral."

"Christine's already told me."

"I know. But last night Dad said he'd also seen him five years ago. He was hanging around Piers' and Mary's house. Dad had decided to let the house and was there to meet the estate agent. He was certain it was one of the boys he'd met years earlier. But when he challenged him, the man said he was mistaken and hurried off."

"So, perhaps he *was* mistaken."

"I don't think so. Dad had all his wits then, very much so. He's vague and rambling now, but if he was certain he recognised someone five years ago you can be damned sure he was right. Dad had a very good memory for faces."

"Did he say which of the boys it was?"

"No. But then he never did know their names." She looked pointedly at her empty glass. "Have I earned another drink?"

"What about making it dinner?"

Her face relaxed in a smile. "Thank you, that would be lovely. But only a bar meal, please. Nothing posh."

"OK, I just have to make a phone call." He stepped off his bar stool and went into the corridor.

"Was that to let your daughter know you'd be late home?" she asked when he returned.

"Yes, it's her turn to get the evening meal."

"Did you tell her you were out with me, or did you say you were working?" she asked lightly.

"Neither, as it happens. Why?"

She looked embarrassed. "I'm sorry … old memories. I shouldn't have asked."

Over the meal later, she said, "You have a very deep voice, you know, George."

Me and Fenella Forman both, Millson thought. "Is that a plus?" he asked.

"Oh, definitely. It's how the female toad selects her mate." She looked at him over her raised wineglass, eyes smiling mischievously. "She chooses the one with the deepest croak because he's older and more experienced, so his genes will give their offspring more chance of survival."

The expression in her eyes changed and George Millson discovered Helen could be as eloquent as Fenella Forman when it came to speaking with her eyes.

The following afternoon Steve Gumbrell parked in the drive of Fenella Forman's house and rang the bell.

"Bring the van up to the house about three, Steve," she'd said that morning. "I'd like you to take some boxes to Coggeshall for me."

Fenella opened the door and pointed to the cardboard boxes in the hall. "That's all my husband's stuff," she said. "I'm sending it back to his family."

After he'd loaded the boxes into the van she handed him a slip of paper. "Here's the address. When you get to the house make sure you deliver them to his stepmother, Christine. I want the bitch to have a good cry over them."

Steve Gumbrell found the address and drove in through the gates and parked in front of the house. Stepping out, he looked up at the gloomy-looking building, wondering what family secrets it held and why Fenella Forman hated her dead husband's stepmother so much.

In the evening, Edward Forman's family gathered in the dining-room of the house to discuss Eddie's future.

"As an in-law," Quentin Page said, taking a seat at the head of the table, "I can be impartial about this. So, I'll kick off, shall I?"

When no one disagreed he adjusted his spectacles and went on, "As I see the situation, the old man is getting steadily worse, and we need to take action now before he becomes completely *non compos mentis*."

"What sort of action?" Helen asked.

"Well, we must obtain power of attorney for a start. It's best to do it now because it'll be much more difficult when he becomes … well, you know …"

"I don't think Eddie will agree to that," said Christine.

"I think he will if the three of you ask him together. You can explain to him it will save him the worry of bills and so on. Ruth tells me the bank has queried his signature a couple of times recently."

"And who would exercise this … this power of attorney?" Christine asked.

"It should be Ruth … she's his eldest."

"And I'm his next of kin," Christine said. "So it should be me."

Quentin looked down his nose at her. "You can hardly expect Ruth and Helen to agree to that, Christine."

"I'll speak for myself, thank you," Helen said curtly. "I want to know what's behind this, Quentin. Whoever has power of attorney will be able to dictate what happens to Dad, won't they?"

"It doesn't work quite like that, Helen." He smiled indulgently. "The power has to be exercised in accordance with his wishes."

"And who decides what his wishes are when he can't tell us for himself?"

"Well … we have to act in his best interests."

"Best interests?" Helen spoke tersely. "Your idea of what's best for him is to put him in a home. That's what's behind this, isn't it?"

"Well … since you bring it up … that *is* something we have to decide."

"*We?*" Helen's voice rose. "You don't have any say in this, Quentin."

"No? And who will be looking after him for the next ten years? You, Helen? Are you going to have him to live with you? Feed him … see to him? Of course you're not! It'll be Ruth. Well, Ruth is my wife, so don't tell me I have no say in this."

"What about me?" Christine demanded. "Don't I have a say too?"

Quentin's lip curled. "Don't tell me you've turned into a loving wife again now Bobby's dead."

"How dare you! I've always—"

"Oh, don't come the innocent with me, Christine. I saw what was going on. The old man lying up there half doped, and you down here carrying on with his son."

"You *bastard!* You filthy-minded bastard!" Christine burst into tears.

"Quentin, for God's sake!" Ruth cried. "Just leave it, will you?"

"No. It's time Eddie was told what's been going on behind his back, because I don't reckon Christine aims to look after him much longer, now she hasn't got Bobby to comfort her."

"Oh, how could you!" Christine wailed. "You're *evil!*" Sobbing, she scrambled to her feet and ran from the room.

Helen stood up. "I don't know what you think you're doing, Quentin, but that was unforgivable. I hope you're proud of yourself." She faced her sister. "I'm sorry for you, Ruth, having a husband like him." She pushed her chair back and made for the door.

"Helen, wait!" Ruth called. "We have to agree what to do about Dad. Please!"

Helen turned. "No, we don't," she said. "Not yet."

She walked out.

Later that night, as Edward Forman lay sleeping, heavily sedated with sleeping pills, the door of his bedroom quietly opened. He slept alone in the double bed. Christine had taken to a room on the other side of the landing two years ago.

The intruder approached the bed, and stood gazing at Eddie lying on his back with his mouth open. After a moment, the intruder poured half a glass of water from the carafe on the bedside table and bending over the sleeping man, gently squeezed his nostrils and poured the water into his mouth; then, quickly replacing the glass, held the old man's mouth and nose closed and tipped his head back. Eddie swallowed and the water went down the open airway into his lungs.

There was no struggle, no threshing about. Frail and sedated, Eddie Forman died quickly, the fluid in his lungs causing a sudden acute heart failure.

Sixteen

The next morning Millson had an unexpected phone call from his solicitor. "I've had a letter from your ex-wife's solicitors, George. She's going to apply for a court order requiring you to return Dena to her."

"But she's already tried that once and lost."

"She didn't lose. She dropped the case because she was having a baby and because your daughter reacted somewhat violently to the Court Welfare officers when they tried to persuade her to return."

"Yes, and she'll do the same again."

"Maybe so. But last time Dena had only been with you a short while and the Welfare people had nothing to go on except her reaction, so they left things as they were after Jean dropped the case. We'll have to wait and see why she's starting it up again. As soon as I hear I'll give you a ring and we'll arrange an appointment."

Millson put down the phone, stunned by the news. He couldn't believe it. There had been no warning, no discussion. But his former wife had never been one for discussion. When Dena first came to him Jean had snapped down the phone, "She can stay till the end of the school holidays. No longer."

"But she's brought her clothes and she says she's come for good," he said. "She doesn't want to live with you, she wants to live with me."

"Don't argue, George. If she's not back here by the time school starts you'll be in trouble." With that his ex had slammed down the phone.

Despite her threat nothing had happened for several months. Then she had gone to court and there had been a visit from the Court Welfare officers. Dena had told them they'd have to put her in a straitjacket to get her back to her mother and stepfather and she'd walk out again as soon as they took it off. After that his ex-wife had apparently dropped the case, and Dena told him her mother was having a baby and wasn't interested in her any more.

Later in the morning the report of the Strathclyde police's further interview with Sean Kebble's mother arrived on Millson's desk. Tracy Kebble said she had no idea where Sean was and was as anxious as the police to find him. She'd last heard from him two months before and was convinced something had happened to him because he had hadn't phoned her on her birthday, as he'd promised. Enclosed with the report was a description of her son and a copy of the only photograph Mrs Kebble had of him.

Millson gazed at the faded photograph of a young man of about twenty-five wearing a suit. These were the times he most missed a smoke … when he wanted to think. Once he would have lit a cigarette, sat back, and let his thoughts wander over possibilities. Delving in his drawer for a barley sugar, he peeled off the paper and popped the lump in his mouth.

Scobie looked up as Millson loomed over him later. "That corpse on Dengie. Where's the photograph of the face they took at the post-mortem?"

"In the case file."

"Bring it to me." Millson stumped out.

When Scobie returned he found Millson sitting at his desk peering at another photograph through a magnifying glass. "Ah, Sherlock Holmes is alive and well in Colchester," he said jokingly.

"Save the wit for your girlfriend, Norris." Millson snatched the post-mortem photo from him and studied it. Then he picked up the one on his desk and handed them both to Scobie. "What d'you think?" he asked.

Scobie held the two pictures side by side and examined them critically. "I wouldn't say they're of the same person, if that's what you're thinking," he said.

"Even assuming a twenty-year difference in age?"

Scobie shook his head doubtfully.

Millson sighed. "I was afraid you'd say that."

"Mind you, the post-mortem photo is pretty gruesome," Scobie said. "He wouldn't look like that in life. Who's the lad in the suit?"

"Sean Kebble."

"Why should it be him?" Scobie asked.

"Only that he came from this area originally, and according to his mother he's been missing for about two months."

"Maybe he's lying low because we've issued an appeal for him," Scobie suggested.

"That's possible. But I'm going to play a wild card, Norris. Fix up for Mrs Kebble to come down and take a look at our unknown."

"She won't be very happy coming all this way if it isn't her son."

"She'll be even less happy if it is," Millson said.

Helen Forman phoned at midday. She was almost incoherent as she told him of her father's sudden death. Interrupting his words of sympathy, she said their distress had been made worse by the family doctor. Christine Forman had sent for him when she found her husband dead in bed that morning.

"He won't give a death certificate," Helen said. "It's ridiculous! Dad died peacefully in the night. It was heart failure – the doctor says so himself. But he's refused to issue a certificate, and he's reported the death to the coroner. Can he do that, George?"

"Did he give a reason?" Millson asked.

"He told Christine he'd only been treating Dad for Alzheimer's disease, and that was not the cause of his heart failure. What does that matter?"

Millson thought the doctor was being over-cautious. A doctor can certify death as natural if he attended the deceased during his last illness, and saw him within fourteen days before or after death. He believed most doctors would have issued a certificate without question in Edward Forman's case.

"Legally, he's within his rights," he told her.

"I don't understand. Christine said there was froth around Dad's mouth. That's a clear sign of heart failure in elderly people and, anyway, the doctor thinks so too."

"That was his mode of dying, Helen, not the cause of death," Millson said. He thought Helen should have known that, being a nurse. "Presumably, the doctor didn't expect his heart to fail."

"So, what happens now?"

"The coroner will order a post-mortem."

"Oh no! We've suffered enough without that." She sounded near to tears.

"It's routine in these cases, Helen. I expect your GP's just covering himself. Try not to worry."

Millson told Scobie that Eddie Forman had died in the night as they had their usual lunch of beer and sandwiches in the Red Lion.

"Poor old chap," Scobie said. "A welcome release for him, though."

"There'll be a PM."

"Oh, why?"

"Just his GP covering himself, I think."

Tracy Kebble came down by train overnight. She was met at Euston and taken to Maldon in a police car, arriving at the mortuary soon after Millson and Scobie. Millson was taken aback by the sad-looking sixty-year-old with a motherly face. She didn't at all fit Alice Tolley's description of a wayward young girl who'd passed her illegitimate son off as her brother.

Mrs Kebble politely declined Scobie's offer of a cup of tea, saying she would rather get her ordeal over first. In the viewing room she gazed through the viewing window at the sheeted body lying on the mortuary trolley. An attendant peeled back the sheet to reveal the face and she stared at it for a long time. As Millson was about to touch her arm and ask if it was her son, she suddenly uttered a loud wail and he knew. Sean Kebble couldn't have responded to their appeal for him even if he'd wanted to. He'd died weeks before, drowned on the mudflats at Dengie.

It was only by chance the body had been still available for viewing. The Rochford District Coroner had inserted the statutory notices in newspapers and circulated other coroners' districts, as he was required to do by law, and decided the deceased could not be identified. He'd closed the inquest, returned a verdict of misadventure and informed the Registrar of Deaths and the local council. If the local council had not been so slow, they would have collected the body by now and buried it in an unmarked grave at public expense.

Millson escorted the distraught Mrs Kebble to the mortuary office and Scobie brought her tea. Amid all her distress Millson could not but feel quietly pleased that his wild card had paid off.

After she had recovered a little Tracy Kebble wanted to know how and where her son died. When Scobie told her he'd been found drowned on the Essex mudflats she cried out, "Drowned? Sean hated the sea! He couldn't swim. What was he doing there?"

Millson said gently, "That's what we'd like to know, Mrs Kebble, and we're hoping you can help us."

She had little enough information to give them. She didn't know where Sean lived, or what he was doing in Essex. And she had no idea what he did for money, although she feared whatever it was would be illegal. She thought this was probably the reason no one else had reported his disappearance.

She said sadly, "I'm afraid Sean wasn't very honest, Mr Millson, never has been. But he was my son and I loved him. So I didn't ask questions. I was just glad to have him phone now and again and let me know he was OK."

Millson nodded sympathetically. "How old was your son, Mrs Kebble?"

Her eyes filled with tears. "He'd have been forty-three next birthday." She ferreted in her handbag for tissues and wiped her eyes.

"I know this is upsetting for you, Mrs Kebble," Millson said. "But we need every scrap of information we can get to find out how your son died. Now, I gather he told you he and Barry Naylor were friends years ago and they were together in a hostel in Wickford after Barry absconded from Mr and Mrs Forman. Can you recall him mentioning their other foster children, Alan Stigall and Sandra Mitchell?"

She shook her head. "Sorry. He just said that about Barry in passing, like. Never spoke about him or the others before."

As she was leaving, after completing the formalities for claiming her son's body, she turned to Millson and said, "I've just remembered. The last time he phoned me – that'd be two months ago – he said he was in Leeds."

Driving back to Colchester, Millson wondered if Sean had been visiting Sandra Mitchell in Leeds. Was that why she fled? And why was he in Essex? To blackmail someone?

"Get on to Delayney's agent again, Norris. This is a murder inquiry now. Tell him unless I have an explanation of what Delayney's yacht was doing at the murder scene within the next seven days, I'll apply for a warrant for his client's arrest."

"We're definitely treating Sean Kebble's death as murder, then?" Scobie asked in surprise.

163

"No, suspicious. But Delayney's agent will move faster if there's a risk of his client's name being linked to a murder case."

Back at his office Millson called in the press liaison officer and dictated a press release. In it, he said a body found on Dengie Flats on the twenty-first of June had now been identified as that of Sean Kebble, aged forty-three. The police were treating his death as suspicious and were anxious to hear from anyone with information about him and, in particular, about how he came to be in such a remote spot.

"See the nationals get this too, not just the locals," he told the press officer.

He was none too hopeful of a result from the appeal. If, as his mother believed, Sean Kebble was mixed up in shady dealings and criminal activity, it was unlikely any information would be forthcoming from that quarter. However, the incident room team now had a name for the body on Dengie and could carry out further checks of DVLC records, electoral registers and DSS records, which should give leads to follow. The man must have existed somewhere.

He thought about Kebble's connections with Great Yeldham, where the other body had been found. Sean had become friends with one of Mr and Mrs Forman's foster children when the family were living in Wickford. He must surely have encountered the other two at some time before they moved to Great Yeldham.

Millson's thoughts switched to Gordon Delayney. He'd spent time in the village as a boy. Sean had lived there with his mother until he was eighteen. Had the two known each other? And then there was old Eddie Forman. He'd had connections with Great Yeldham too; the body was in his brother's garden and he'd inherited the house.

On a sudden new thought Millson jumped up and went next door to Scobie. "Find out when the PM's being done on Eddie Forman, Norris."

"Why the sudden interest in that?" Scobie asked.

"Apart from the victim and the killer, there were three people who might have known about the murder at Great Yeldham: Sandra Mitchell, Sean Kebble and Eddie Forman. Two of them are now dead."

"But surely old Eddie's death was due to natural causes."

"Sod's law says it won't have been, Norris. Which is why we're going to the post-mortem."

Dr Shepherd was surprised to find a chief inspector and a sergeant from the Essex Constabulary present at his autopsy on Edward Forman, but he made no comment. He was a short, tubby man, bald except for a narrow band of grey bristles round the back of his head from one ear to the other.

Scalpel in hand, he approached the body lying on the mortuary slab with the genial expression of a butcher about to carve a slice of prime beef for a customer. Deftly, he sliced open the corpse from neck to pubis, detouring the tough tissue of the navel which would have been difficult to cut and even more difficult to sew up again. As he worked, he dictated to an overhead microphone. After a while he stopped and turned to Millson.

"Fluid in the lungs, Chief Inspector. When the heart stops pumping, water accumulates in the lungs ... typically so in deaths of elderly patients with heart trouble."

"So, nothing suspicious, then?" Millson asked, his spirits rising.

"I'm afraid there is," said Dr Shepherd. "This man's lungs contain a good deal more fluid than I would expect, and there's nothing wrong with his heart. On the contrary, it is in good condition for a man of his age."

"So, what was the cause of death?"

"There are really only two possibilities: drowning and drug overdose – the post-mortem condition is much the same in each case. If you come across an apparent case of drowning on the roof of a tower block it's likely to be the result of a drug overdose. And if you have a senior citizen on heart pills dying at home you suspect cardiac arrest." He stripped off his surgical gloves.

"Isn't that the case here?" Millson wondered why the pathologist felt it necessary to expand on the subject.

Dr Shepherd shook his head. "No. This man was not on medication and his heart was perfectly sound."

Millson was becoming frustrated. "So, what are you saying, Doctor?"

Dr Shepherd brought the tips of his fingers together and placed them beneath his chin, his expression avuncular. "I think he drowned."

Millson goggled at him. "How can a man drown in bed in his own house?"

The doctor dropped his hands and smiled briefly. "Not by accident, obviously."

"Murder?" Millson asked incredulously. "How?"

Scobie saw Dr Shepherd's face assume the sort of expression Millson's did when he was about to drag up some previous case that seemed relevant. "Vienna 1989, Chief Inspector. A serial killer – a hospital nurse, of all people – admitted drowning twenty elderly patients while they were sleeping by holding their nostrils and pouring water down their throats. The water goes straight down into the lungs causing almost instant heart failure. It's a quick death and, from the criminal aspect, leaves no trace because water in the lungs of an elderly person is considered normal."

Scobie glanced covertly at Millson. He looked stunned. "I've never heard of it," he said.

"Well, no, you wouldn't have," the doctor said in a patronising tone. "The case didn't go to trial. It was only reported in the medical journals."

"And is this what you're going to say in your report? Someone poured water down his throat and drowned him?"

Dr Shepherd's face wore a pained expression. "You know better than that, Chief Inspector. I shall give the cause of death as fluid in the lungs causing heart failure. I shall report that I found no physiological explanation of the water in his lungs, and venture an opinion on ways it might have come about. It will be up to the coroner what action he takes."

Millson was silent for a moment. Then he said, "There is another possibility, you know, Doctor."

"Really? And what is that?"

"Burking," Millson said.

"I beg your pardon?"

"Named after Burke and Hare – the Edinburgh body-snatchers. One held the victim down while the other sat on the chest and put his hand over the nose and mouth. It's quick and effective, causes heart failure, and leaves no trace," Millson said, looking pleased with himself.

"I don't think I've heard of those cases," Dr Shepherd said.

"Well, no, you wouldn't have," Millson said, with a

straight face. "They happened in the early 1800s. But you'll find the cases referred to in crime journals."

"I don't think it's relevant here," said Dr Shepherd. "It takes two people to do that and I would expect to find signs of bruising."

"Not if the victim happened to be sedated," Millson said. "Edward Forman's wife gave him sleeping pills every night."

"I see. Thank you," Dr Shepherd said. "I'll mention the possibility in my report – though I certainly shan't call it Burking."

Seventeen

Superintendent Kitchen looked puzzled when he called Millson to his office the following morning to tell him the coroner had asked for inquiries to be made into the death of Edward Forman. "What's going on, George? We've had a skeleton in the daughter's garden, the son's died in suspicious circumstances, and now there's something fishy about the father's death. Is there a connection?"

"Not that I can see at the moment," Millson said.

"Damned unlucky family, then, that's all I can say." Superintendent Kitchen opened the cigarette box on his desk and offered it to Millson. "Oh, I forgot ... you've given up," he said as Millson shook his head.

Millson doubted whether he'd forgotten. Kitchen was one of those heavy smokers who make a practice of offering cigarettes to ex-smokers.

The superintendent lit a cigarette and exhaled smoke over him. "What's the state of play on this body on Dengie you've just identified? Good work that, by the way. Was that Scobie?"

"No, sir. It was me. Norris takes the credit for tracing the yacht. It belongs to an actor called Gordon Delayney. He's out of the country at present and we're trying to contact him."

"Good man, Scobie. Knew he'd find it," Kitchen said effusively. "Well, keep me posted. I don't like all these loose ends."

"Neither do I," Millson said irritably.

"Who first?" Scobie asked when Millson told him they were going to interview Eddie Forman's family. "His wife? She found the body."

"It's not that kind of inquiry, Norris. Eddie wasn't found with his head bashed in. As far as the family know, he died peacefully in bed during the night. So, we won't go charging in bombarding them with questions. A tactful approach is what's needed here. We'll have a chat with Helen to start with."

In Great Yeldham Helen Forman looked surprised to see the two of them when she opened her front door. Millson had left a message at the hospital saying he would call that evening, and he realised she'd assumed it was a social call and he'd be alone. When he saw the tray of drinks and dishes of nibbles set out in the sitting-room, he felt guilty for not making his message more explicit.

"What is it? What's happened?" she asked as they sat down.

"Nothing's happened, Helen," Millson said. "It's just that the doctor who did the post-mortem on your father can't decide exactly how he died, and the coroner has asked us to make some inquiries."

She frowned. "But Christine says the coroner's office has issued a burial certificate and we can go ahead with the funeral. Doesn't that mean everything is all right?"

"There will still be an inquest to help the coroner determine how your father came by his death," he explained. "And that's why we're here. We'd like to ask you some questions."

"I see." She looked down at the floor. "So, what do you want to ask me?"

"First, the routine question we always ask. Where were you the night he died between, say, ten o'clock and four o'clock the following morning?" Dr Shepherd had been unwilling to be any more precise about the time of death.

"I was at Dad's house until about half-past eleven. We had a family meeting that evening to discuss what to do about him. It developed into a slanging match between Quentin and Christine. Sad, wasn't it? Dad upstairs in bed, us downstairs arguing about him." She turned her head away.

"So, when did you last see him?"

"About half-past eleven when I went up to kiss him goodbye." She faced him again, her eyes glistening. "He was asleep. After that I came home and went to bed."

He nodded. "And the other question I have to ask is, who benefits from your father's death?"

"Under his will, you mean? We all do. He's left the house to Ruth – with Christine having a life interest in it. My mortgage on this house is to be paid off and half the rest of the money goes to Christine. The other half is divided equally between Ruth and me, now that Bobby's dead."

"Thank you, Helen." Millson stood up.

She looked up at him. "Is that all, then … George?"

"Yes, that's fine."

It wasn't. He'd hoped to eliminate her from suspicion.

But she'd not only been in the house, she had actually gone up to her father's room while he was asleep in bed.

"Well, I'd say we can rule her out," Scobie said cheerfully, as they drove away. "She was really upset."

"Oh, she was upset all right," Millson said moodily. "Doesn't mean she's innocent, though."

"Why on earth not?"

Millson said patiently, "Hasn't it occurred to you this could be a mercy killing, Norris?" As Scobie stared at him he went on, "The old man knew he was getting worse and he'd soon be unable to feed himself … need help to go to the toilet … and suffer God knows what other indignities. Wouldn't it be natural for a loving daughter to spare him all that? A daughter who's a nurse and knows how to help him into the next world without risk to herself. Oh no, we can't rule out Helen Forman simply because she's devastated by what she's done."

Scobie was aghast. "She wouldn't do a thing like that!"

"No? Not if he'd begged her to? Because he did, you know. She as good as told me so the evening we had dinner in the Red Lion."

"Oh." Scobie stared through the windscreen, his cheerfulness gone.

The other members of the family were interviewed at the Coggeshall house in the morning. Millson began with Ruth Page and her husband. Their L-shaped bed-sitting room at the back of the house seemed even more cramped on this second visit.

Ruth Page greeted them nervously, her pale face strained with lines of sadness. "I expect you'd like to speak to us separately, Chief Inspector," she said. "I'll be in the big room at the front when you need me." She moved past him and out of the door.

"What did they find at the post-mortem?" Quentin Page asked, as Millson and Scobie took chairs from the dining alcove and sat down.

"It was inconclusive," Millson said.

"Suspicious, eh?" Page looked pleased.

"Inconclusive," Millson repeated firmly. "So, we're here to enquire into the way Mr Forman died and clear things up."

"OK." Page shrugged his shoulders and lay back in his chair with his hands clasped together. "Enquire away."

"I understand there was an argument at a meeting here the evening your father-in-law died," Millson said. "What was that about?"

"I suppose Helen told you." Page fingered his moustache. "I was trying to get the family to make a sensible decision about Eddie. I suggested Ruth – as the elder daughter – should have power of attorney over her father's affairs so we could have access to his money and settle him in a nursing home. Christine argued she was the one who should have power of attorney, and Helen refused to even consider putting Eddie in a home. She seemed to think the rest of us should just go on coping with him. It was totally unreasonable to expect us to put up with a senile old man who could live for another twenty years or more."

"Convenient, then, his dying in the night like that," Millson said.

"Oh, yes." Page smiled unpleasantly. "Especially for Christine."

"Why her especially?"

"If Eddie had lived, he'd have altered his will, and she'd have been a great deal worse off when he died." There was a malevolent expression on Page's face.

Millson frowned. "Why should Mr Forman do that to his wife?"

Page curled his lip. "She'd been carrying on with his son, Bobby, that's why. Here in his own house … right under his nose."

"You mean they were having an affair?"

"Affair? They were lovers!" He looked at Millson and then at Scobie. "You don't seemed shocked," he said accusingly.

"Should we be?" Millson asked. "These things happen."

"Not between stepmother and stepson, they don't! It's a prohibited relationship. You read your Bible. Leviticus Twenty. 'A man that lieth with his father's wife hath uncovered his father's nakedness and both of them shall surely be put to death.' That's what it says." Quentin Page's eyes gleamed fanatically.

"Very few people take the Bible literally, Mr Page."

"Not about putting to death maybe, but up to a few years ago the law forbade a stepson and stepmother to marry or have sex. And for the same reason as the Bible gives. It's incest!"

Scobie looked up from note-taking. "Eddie didn't know about the affair, though. So why would he alter his will, Mr Page?"

"I was going to tell him."

"What on earth for? It's over. His son's dead," Scobie said.

"Because it was time he knew what sort of woman she is!" Page said viciously.

"And if Eddie had altered his will, more money would have come to your wife, of course," Scobie said.

"That had nothing to do with it!" Page retorted. "Christine was sleeping with his son. She shouldn't have been allowed to get away with it."

"Did Mrs Forman know you were going to tell on her?" Millson asked.

"Yes, I said so at the meeting. That's why she ducked out of it. Next thing you know the old man's dead."

"Are you accusing Mrs Forman of murdering her husband, Mr Page?" Millson asked sternly.

"I'm simply pointing out facts."

"But do you have any evidence she killed him?"

"No, of course I don't," Page snapped. "That's why you're making enquiries, isn't it? And I'm telling you she's the one with the motive."

"Yes. Thank you for that," Millson said dryly. "Let's return to the evening before his death. I'd like to be clear on the sequence of events. What time did this family meeting end?"

"About half ten. Helen and Christine went off to the kitchen, and Ruth and I went on talking in the dining-room. We heard Christine go upstairs about eleven. Then Helen looked in to say she was going, and went upstairs to say goodbye to Eddie. She left about ten minutes later and Ruth and I went to bed soon after."

"Did you hear anything in the night? Anyone moving about?"

"No, but then we wouldn't from this part of the house. Eddie's bedroom's at the front, and so is Christine's."

"Thank you, Mr Page. Perhaps you'd ask your wife to come in now."

Page nodded and went out of the door.

"Wonder why he's so keen to point the finger at Christine?" Scobie asked.

"Same reason he wanted her out of the will," Millson said. "If she were convicted of murdering her husband she'd couldn't inherit under his will and that would leave more for Ruth."

Ruth Page entered and sat down in the armchair. When Millson explained the post-mortem result she seemed unconcerned. "Doctors don't know everything, do they?" she said. "I suppose because he couldn't find out exactly why Dad died he's making a mystery out of it."

"Unfortunately, Ruth, that means the police have to make sure there were no suspicious circumstances."

"Suspicious? How could there be? Dad died in his sleep."

"Quite so. But we have to consider every possibility, and your husband has made allegations against your stepmother which he intended repeating to your father. Did you know about these?"

"About her and Bobby, you mean? Yes … well, not in detail." Ruth Page dropped her eyes in embarrassment. "Quentin is very moral, you see. He – um …" She hesitated. "Well, he considered Christine had committed a terrible sin and should be punished."

Scobie asked, "What about the effect on your poor father?"

She looked down at her hands. "Yes, I know. I begged him not to say anything, but he said we all have a duty to uphold the sanctity of marriage. He's very moral, you see," she repeated lamely, apparently unable to think of another excuse.

Millson suddenly felt sorry for her. "Would you mind telling me your movements the evening your father died, Ruth? Starting from ten-thirty."

"I was in the dining-room then with Quentin – the main one, that is – trying to persuade him not to upset Dad. I heard Christine go upstairs to put Dad to bed as usual. Then when Helen left – sometime after eleven, I think – I came back here and went to bed."

"And your husband too?"

"No. Quentin was tidying the dining-room after the meeting, and locking up the house. He came to bed later."

"You didn't go upstairs and say goodnight to your father?" Millson hoped Helen was not the only person to have visited Eddie after he went to bed.

"Like Helen, you mean? No." She gave a faint smile. "Helen liked to make up for not seeing him as often as I did."

"You didn't hear anything during the night? No unexpected sounds? No one moving about."

"No."

"Could anyone have entered the house without your knowing?"

"Not unless they had keys. This house is very secure."

"Does anyone apart from you and your husband, and Christine, have keys?"

"Only Helen. And Bobby had a set, of course. Fenella ought to return them now, I suppose."

"Well, thank you for your help, Ruth." Millson stood up. "Where can we find Christine?"

"She'll be in the small sitting-room, I expect. It's the next door to ours along the hall."

It was the room where they had interviewed Christine

after Bobby Forman's funeral. This time there was no misery or signs of crying on her face when she opened the door to Millson's knock.

"I've no doubt Quentin will have already told you Eddie was murdered and I did it," she said calmly as they took seats.

"That wasn't quite how he put it," Millson said cautiously. "But it was certainly what he implied."

"And he'll have told you about me and Bobby, of course. Fenella chose the perfect accomplice for her dirty work."

"Fenella? I'm afraid you've lost me, Mrs Forman."

She said bitterly, "Oh, Fenella got her revenge all right."

"I still don't follow," Millson said.

"On Eddie, for shaming her in front of everyone at the funeral. And on me because Bobby loved me. She found my letters, and sent them to Quentin. He was going to show them to Eddie and tell him we'd been lovers and he'd seen us—" She broke off and looked away. "He came to my room that night and blackmailed me."

"Let me get this clear," Millson said. "You're saying that on the night your husband died, Mr Page came to your room and threatened you?"

"Oh, yes. He enjoyed doing it too."

Eighteen

She had been undressed and ready for bed when the tap came at her door.

"Who is it?"

"Quentin. I want to speak to you."

She slipped a dressing-gown over her night-dress and opened the door. "What do you want?"

"I've got some letters of yours." He pushed his way in and closed the door. "Fenella found them when she went through Bobby's things. She wants me to read them to his father."

"Oh God ... no." Christine sank down on the bed, stunned. She recovered herself. "You're not going to do it, surely?" When he didn't answer, just continued looking at her, she said urgently, "Please, Quentin, you can't. However much you dislike me, you can't. They're silly letters I wrote. They're just ... affectionate."

"They're *love* letters, Christine. They may not actually mention sex, but reading between the lines it's obvious you were having it off with him. And I saw you together. You were—"

"You saw *nothing!*"

"Oh, yes, I did. Kissing and cuddling. The point is, Christine, Eddie will believe whatever I tell him about you when I've read these letters to him."

"He won't understand what you're talking about. You'll simply upset him. That's cruel."

"Oh, he'll understand all right. He still has his good days when he's with it, even if his memory's going. Then a few words from Ruthie ... and he'll alter his will. Cut you out. Everything will go to her and Helen, and you'll get nothing."

"You're *wicked!* Why are you doing this to me?"

"I won't if you persuade Eddie to give Ruth power of attorney – which he will if *you* ask him. Then you can have your letters back, and I'll keep quiet about you and Bobby."

She stared at him, frowning. "And then what?"

"We put Eddie in a home where he'll be properly cared for, give you enough of his capital to buy a flat, and Ruth and I will have this house. You'll still get your third share of what's left when he dies."

"How do I know you won't have milked it long before then?"

"You'll just have to trust me."

"What about my monthly allowance?"

"That'll have to stop. You'll be able to take a job when you haven't got Eddie and the house to look after."

Christine bit her lip. "If Ruth has control of her father's affairs – which means you will, really – I'll have no security. No guarantee you'll do what you say. I want something in writing."

He shook his head. "You're in no position to bargain, Christine."

"This is blackmail!"

"Call it what you like." He took a step forward, standing over her menacingly as she sat on the bed. "You're a whore, Christine, an incestuous whore. And an adulteress. You've brought this on yourself."

"You hypocrite!" She jumped up and pushed him away from her. "You bloody hypocrite!" she said fiercely. "This isn't about my morals. It's about turning me out of the house and getting your hands on Eddie's money."

He said angrily, "That's enough! I've offered you a deal – which is more than you deserve. Take it or leave it." He turned towards the door.

"I need time to think."

"You've got time," he said nastily. "All night."

Recounting the scene to Millson, Christine said, "And now I suppose you think I killed my husband to prevent it happening?"

He said gravely, "It's a possibility I have to consider, Mrs Forman."

"Eddie was dead when I found him," she insisted. "He was cold. He must have died in the night while we were all asleep."

"I'm interested in an earlier time for the moment," Millson said. "You put him to bed about ten-thirty, I understand."

"Yes."

"And gave him his sleeping pills as usual?"

"Ye-es." She hesitated, then her shoulders rose and fell in a sigh. "I suppose Helen has told you I gave him extra that night."

Millson raised his eyebrows. "How much extra?"

"Twice his usual dose. Eddie was very upset that day …

181

far worse than usual. He was rambling again about Piers and Mary's foster son. Said he kept seeing him everywhere. It was all rubbish. But he was so agitated I was afraid he'd get up in the night and wander about. Perhaps fall down the stairs. So I asked Helen if it would be all right to double his dose. She said it would be OK."

Millson looked down at his toecaps. Innocent advice? Or had it given Helen the opportunity she'd been waiting for?

"You drive, Norris. I want to think," Millson said, getting into the passenger seat.

He laid his head against the head rest and ran over the interviews, considering the family one by one. Ruth, elder daughter ... not a serious suspect. Husband, Quentin. Probably capable of murdering for money, but no point when he was about to gain what he wanted by blackmail. Christine. Millson's brows came together. She had most to lose if Eddie lived and most to gain if he died – including not having to look after him any longer. There was only her word for it that Eddie had been in a disturbed state, and that was the reason she'd given him extra sleeping pills. She was also the person who could most easily slip into his room during the night. Yes, if Eddie had been murdered, Christine Forman was a firm suspect. Lastly, Helen.

Millson tried to put aside his liking for her and consider her in the same way as the others. Helen was compassionate and caring, she loved her father and she understood the dreadful prognosis of his disease. Eddie had begged her not to let him be put in a home. And Millson was sure he'd also begged her to end his suffering when the time came. Had Quentin Page's proposal precipitated matters? And was Helen capable of committing a mercy-killing? On balance, he thought she probably was. Her training would have given her the will and the compassion to do it. Would she use the method Dr Shepherd had described, though? It sounded too brutal. But if it was quick and painless, as the doctor said, perhaps she would.

Beside him, Scobie could contain himself no longer. "It has to be the wife, doesn't it? She had to act quickly to pre-empt Page carrying out his threat. And if Eddie's GP hadn't been so pernickety she'd have got away with it."

Millson abandoned his musing and collected his thoughts. "Then why draw attention to herself by asking Helen's advice about sleeping tablets?"

"She had to be sure it was a safe dose. She wanted Eddie comatose, but if she'd overdosed him she'd have been in trouble."

Millson nodded. "Maybe so. Helen is a strong suspect too, though. The trouble is all the evidence is circumstantial, and I haven't a clue where to go from here."

Millson's solicitor phoned in the afternoon to tell him he'd received the papers from his ex-wife's solicitors. "Things look bad, George. I'd like to see you right away if that's possible."

"I'm on my way," Millson said grimly.

This time his ex-wife had assembled a list of allegations against him, the solicitor explained. "Neglect ... lack of care ... abduction—"

"*Abduction?* You're joking."

"One learns not to joke in my business," the solicitor said severely. "Jean has custody of Dena and you had a duty to return her. You didn't, and legally speaking that's abduction. We'll probably dispose of that one without much trouble. It's the allegations of neglect and lack of care we have to worry about."

"But they're nonsense!"

"Unfortunately not. She must have used a private detective. There's a list of times when Dena was left alone in the house late at night and, on occasions, into the early hours of the morning."

"Only when I'm working on a case."

"That's her strongest point. Your work. You're away a lot and you don't have the time to care for Dena properly."

"That's bollocks!" Millson snarled.

"No, George, it's what the court will regard as an important factor," the solicitor said.

"Well, what about Dena in all this? The courts are supposed to take account of children's wishes and act in their best interests, aren't they? And Dena sure as hell doesn't want to go back to her mother."

The solicitor sighed. "Ah, that life were that simple. What a child says it wants and what a court thinks are in its best interests are by no means always the same."

"They can't really take her away, can they? She'd scream the place down."

The solicitor nodded sympathetically. "Even then," he said.

Millson looked at him bleakly. "You've got to stop it."

"I'll do all I can, George. The problem is your ex-wife was granted custody, and you agreed to it at the time of the divorce. She's simply asking the court to enforce that. Have you told Dena?"

"Not yet. I didn't want to upset her."

"Then you'd better do so right away. It's possible a

social worker could descend on you with an order to take her into care."

"*What!*"

"Keep calm. It shouldn't happen, but if it does ring me immediately. I'll go straight to a judge in chambers and have her returned to you until the court case is heard."

"You're sure?"

"In your circumstances, yes. And I know the judge I'd be applying to. Don't worry."

Driving to work next morning Millson was feeling depressed. The previous evening he had faced up to telling his daughter of her mother's new attempt to make her go back.

"Don't worry, Dad, it won't get her anywhere. It'll be like before. I'll tell the Social I won't go and that'll be that."

"Not this time, I'm afraid, love." He gave her an edited version of his meeting with the solicitor. She went quiet and hardly spoke for the rest of the evening. When she went to bed early he'd reached for the whisky bottle.

He arrived at his office and slumped down in his chair feeling drained. The half-bottle of whisky he'd drunk last night was playing havoc with his digestion and he was weary of trying to make sense of the four deaths. At one point, as the whisky began to bite, he'd thought he saw the glimmer of a connection between them all. But it had vanished with the next half tumbler, and he'd continued going round in circles attempting to solve the insoluble.

The phone rang. He very nearly didn't answer, having decided the sensible thing to do was to take the day off and go home. But habit prevailed. "Yes?"

It was one of the desk officers at the front door. "There's a Sandra Mitchell asking to see you, sir."

Millson's lethargy and depression suddenly evaporated. "Bring her up!"

By the time Sandra Mitchell was shown into the room he'd raided his drawer and bolted two large bars of caramel chocolate.

Nineteen

Sandra Mitchell was a tall blonde with large blue eyes. Her hair formed a halo of tight curls around her pert face, and she was not much like the sad, hard-faced women of her profession Millson had encountered in the past. He thought she'd probably have little respect for the police, and decided to keep the interview informal.

He waved to the chair beside his desk and she sat down in a waft of perfume, and unbuttoned her leather coat. Underneath she was wearing a white blouse and light blue pleated skirt.

She delved in her handbag and brought out a packet of cigarettes and a lighter. "OK if I smoke?" she asked, waving a cigarette at him. Her voice was hoarse like someone with laryngitis.

He nodded. Opening a drawer, he took out the ashtray he kept for visitors and pushed it towards her. "Ta." She lit her cigarette, placed the lighter and cigarette packet beside her on Millson's desk, and snapped her bag shut. "I've come here because I read how you found Sean, and you want information about him. All right?"

So it was Sean Kebble's death, not his carefully worded appeal to her, that had brought Sandra Mitchell out of hiding. "I'd like to hear what you know about the body at Great Yeldham first, Sandra," he said.

She inhaled deeply and blew smoke across his desk. "OK. Well, for a start, you got it wrong. It's not Al Stigall, it's Barry Naylor."

Millson relaxed, feeling the tension leaving him. He'd been afraid she knew nothing about the body, only about Sean Kebble. He pushed his chair away from the desk and settled back comfortably. "Take your time and let's have the story from the beginning, Sandra."

"Yeah, OK." She deposited her bag on the desk beside the cigarettes and smoothed her skirt. "Me and Al was put with the Formans when they lived in Wickford. Barry was already there ... he'd been with them a while." She gave a slight smile. "Barry took a bit of a shine to me, he did. And I liked him too. He was nice looking ... and kind of shy." She paused, remembering.

She went on, "Then me foster mum and dad decided to move to Yeldham. Barry didn't want that. He wanted to stay in Wickford and just before we moved he did a runner. He was about sixteen or seventeen so no one bothered much. Before he went, he told me he was going to get a job and come back for me and we'd set up together somewhere. I didn't believe him, of course." She paused again, drawing on her cigarette. "But one afternoon – months later – Barry did come. Mr and Mrs Forman were out shopping.

"I s'pose when Barry found no one in the house he came down the garden looking for me. Anyways, he comes to the old shed they had at the bottom of the garden and opens the door." She reached out and tapped ash from her cigarette into the ashtray. "He found me all right. Al was screwing me."

Millson's eyebrows rose. "But you were only … ?"

"Twelve. And that's only the half of it." Her eyes met his. "I'm his sister."

Millson eyebrows rose higher then came together in a frown. "If you're Alan Stigall's sister, why the different surnames?"

Her mouth twisted. "Different fathers, of course. Mum didn't know much, poor cow, but she knew that much."

He nodded. "So, what happened?"

"Barry went bananas. Shouted and swore at Al and said he'd tell Mr and Mrs Forman. Al went for him and they started fighting. I ran off up the woods and hid. When I sneaked back later, Barry had gone and the Formans still wasn't home. Al told me he'd talked Barry out of telling on us, and he'd calmed down and gone away quietly. Al said I wasn't to say anything about him coming or what happened else we'd both be in trouble and get sent back to the Children's Home. When I didn't hear from Barry no more I just thought he didn't fancy me after he'd seen me with Al. Now I know different, of course." Her mouth drooped at the corners and she stared down at her lap.

Millson said nothing, not wanting to break the thread of her story. After a moment she raised her head and went on, "I told Al he'd got to stop doing me if he wanted me to keep me mouth shut. He did stop for a while. But about a year later he started on me again. I said I wasn't having any and if he didn't leave me alone I'd tell the Social everything, and they'd lock him up. Next thing I knew he scarpered – took off without a word. Haven't seen or heard from him since. But when I saw about the skeleton on telly I knew it had to be Barry, and Al had killed him."

"You didn't actually see him do it, though, did you?" Millson was disappointed. He'd hoped for an eye-witness account.

"No. I know he did, though."

"How?"

She sat back in the chair and crossed her legs. "Innit about time you offered me a drink or something?"

"Tea or coffee?" He reached for the phone.

"Something a bit stronger would be nice." She gave him a knowing smile. "All the coppers I know keep a drop in the cupboard."

It was against the rules, but it happened and he wondered how many times she'd seen the inside of a police station.

She saw him hesitating. "C'mon," she said. "I won't snitch."

He stood up and went to his cupboard. The whisky bottle only came out on the rare occasions of a celebration with senior officers, and it annoyed him to think she'd now lump him with the other policemen she knew, some of whom were probably clients. That happened too. The information she was giving him was crucial, though and it was vital to maintain her goodwill.

"Tell me how you know Al killed Barry," he said as he set half a tumbler of whisky and a bottle of still water in front of her.

"Ta." She carefully topped up the whisky with an equal amount of water. "A coupla days before Barry come, me foster dad had dug out the lawn in front of the patio so he could make the patio bigger. I saw the photos in the paper and I reckon that's where Al buried Barry while I was up in the woods. Next day, a concrete-mixer lorry come and they run a pipe across the garden and slopped concrete over that bit. Then me dad levelled and smoothed it."

Millson leaned forward. "You're sure this was the day after Barry came to see you?"

"Yeah, I'm sure."

"This fight Al had with Barry. Was he using a weapon of any kind?"

"Not when I ran off. But there was tools in the shed so I 'spect he grabbed one and hit Barry with it." She took another cigarette from the packet, lit it from the tip of the one she'd been smoking and stubbed the end in the ashtray.

Millson watched her thoughtfully. Sandra Mitchell had an open, friendly face and she sounded sincere. But the ready way she speculated on how her half-brother had killed and buried Barry bothered him. According to her, she hadn't actually witnessed any of it and he wondered if she was as innocent and uninvolved as she made out.

"Why didn't you come forward and tell us all this before, Sandra? Why did you run away?"

"Because Sean come to see me. He wanted to know what happened to Barry. Him and Barry were mates, see?"

Sean Kebble was older than Barry, and treated him like a younger brother, she explained, and it was through Barry that Sean came to know her and Alan Stigall. One day, after the family had moved to Yeldham, Barry told Sean he was going there to collect her and they were going to hitch-hike as far away as they could and Sean probably wouldn't hear from him for a while.

"All these years Sean thought Barry and me was happy together somewhere. When he read about the body he knew it was Barry's and he come looking for me. He said he'd smash me face in if I didn't tell him what happened. When

I did, he said he was going to find Al and make him suffer for what he'd done. So, Al would know I'd gabbed and I knew he'd kill me for it. So I hopped it quick. No way was I going to the police. Then when I saw about Sean I knew Al had killed him and I had to do something before he got to me."

Millson nodded. It sounded plausible enough. "Right." He straightened in his chair. "You've been a great help, Sandra, a very great help. Now I want you to repeat everything you've told me to a policewoman, and she'll write it down for you to sign. All right?"

"Yeah, OK."

While she was making her statement Millson ran over her story in his mind. It was clear now why there had been no response from the three foster children. Sandra was in fear of her life, Barry was dead, and Alan Stigall was his killer. One thing puzzled him, though. Apart from Sean Kebble, whose silence was understandable, why had no one else come forward about Stigall? There must be people who'd known him over the last twenty years or so. Of course, poor old Eddie thought he'd seen him – it would have to be Al because Barry was dead – and— Suddenly, the truth hit Millson like an electric shock. *Stigall had changed his name!* Probably done so years ago after he murdered Barry. Eddie *had* seen him at his son's funeral. And the reason police checks on the mourners hadn't uncovered him was because they were searching for an Alan Stigall.

He went next door to Scobie and briefly recounted Sandra Mitchell's story. At the end he said, "Find out about Eddie Forman's funeral, Norris. I want her there."

Scobie gaped. "What for?"

"Eddie was right when he said he'd recognised one of the foster boys at his son's funeral. It had to be Alan Stigall, so

Stigall must be among the friends, acquaintances or associates of the Forman family. In which case there's every chance he'll turn up at Eddie Forman's funeral too."

Scobie frowned. "Then why haven't we come across him?"

"Because he changed his name years ago and we don't know what he looks like," Millson said triumphantly. "And with Mr and Mrs Forman, Sean Kebble and Eddie Forman all dead the only person left who can identify him is Sandra. That's why I want her at Eddie's funeral. She's our only living witness, Norris."

The WDC returned with Sandra Mitchell half an hour later. "She's made a full statement, sir, but she refuses to give her address," the WDC said.

"Didn't the desk sergeant get it from you when you arrived?" Millson asked Sandra.

She gave a crooked smile. "Think I'm simple or something? I gave him me old address in Leeds."

"So, where are you living now?"

The baby-blue eyes narrowed. "Forget it. Soon as you let on to the papers I've come forward, he'll be able to find me easy. And it won't be to give me a hug and a kiss, neither."

"We'll protect you."

"Round the clock? Do me a favour. Couldn't do no business then, could I? Best protection you can give me is not to let on I've been here."

"We won't. But we must be able to contact you, Sandra. I can't let you leave here without knowing where to reach you."

"It's not on," she said. "I'm not giving me address to no one."

Millson's voice hardened. "You're a material witness, and I'll lock you up if I have to. You certainly won't do any business then."

"You can't do that!"

"Watch me," Millson said, lifting his phone.

"No!" Her eyes widened in panic. Then, as he continued holding the phone, "OK, OK! But it's bleeding blackmail, and if I wake up dead one morning, it'll be your sodding fault, OK?"

"Write it down for me," Millson said, unmoved. He pushed a pad and pencil towards her. She leaned down and wrote slowly in capitals. He glanced at the address then tore off the sheet and handed it to the WDC. "Check it out. Make sure it's genuine and she's living there."

"You rotten sod," Sandra said.

"D'you want to change it?"

She shook her head. He nodded to the WDC and she went out. Sandra sat down beside his desk again. "You're a right bastard," she said. "You've got what you want and now you don't care a bugger what happens to me."

"Oh, but I do. I care very much. You're my only hope of finding Alan Stigall. Would you still recognise him after all this time?"

"Oh, yeah, I'd know him all right."

"Good. I want you to come to a funeral."

"What for?" she said. "Funerals give me the creeps."

"To point Alan out to us if he turns up."

She rounded her eyes. "Oh, that's nice! You want me as bait so you can nick him while he's bashing me head in!"

"I'll be right beside you, Sandra, with my sergeant the other side."

"You'd better be," she said sourly. "And you'd better

194

cuff him quick. I don't want me face marked. Anyways, what makes you think he'll come to this funeral?"

"We think he has some connection with the family. We believe he was at the son's funeral a while back, and he probably went to your foster parents' funerals six years ago."

"Don't be daft!" she said scathingly. "That wouldn't be Al. They meant bugger all to him."

"Oh, it wasn't to mourn them. I believe he wanted an excuse to see the patio and make sure it was still intact."

"That figures," she said, looking thoughtful. A moment later she shook her head. "No, I'm not doing it. Suppose Al does come and I don't spot him. He'll know I was there to finger him and he'll kill me for sure later, when you're not around."

"You have to do it, Sandra. You're our only hope of catching him and you'll never be safe until we do. Trust me. We'll take good care of you."

She pursed her lips, considering. "All right," she said at last. "And you better had."

There was a knock at the door and the WPC entered. "Address checks out, sir. She's working the Kings Cross area calling herself Michelle."

Sandra's eyes flashed. "There! Didn't tell you no lies, did I?"

At a press conference later, Millson told reporters the skeleton found in the garden at Great Yeldham was now known to be that of a youth called Barry Naylor and he was anxious to hear from anyone who had known him. Also, he wanted to speak urgently to a man named Alan Stigall, aged thirty-seven, and who might be living under a different name. Anyone with information as to his present whereabouts, or who had known him at any time, should contact the police immediately.

"Is this man a suspect, Chief Inspector?" a reporter asked.

"He is until we can speak to him and eliminate him from our inquiries," Millson said.

"What about the girl, Sandra Mitchell? Have you found her?"

"No, we're still looking for her," Millson said.

When he arrived home that evening Dena was in the sitting-room listening to a CD. He'd asked her what she wanted for her birthday, and she told him a compact disc player, but he'd been doubtful. "You'd be shut away in your room every evening listening to it," he said.

"Not if you flashed out a bit extra and bought headphones as well," she'd said quickly. "Then I could listen down here without disturbing you."

Now she was sitting on the sofa with what looked like large ear muffs clamped either side of her head, rocking back and forth like a disturbed mental patient.

He waved hullo to her and she took them off. "Don't have to worry about the custody case any more, Dad," she said cheerfully. "Mum's dropping it."

"How do you know?"

"I phoned Ted."

It took him a second or two to realise she meant the man who'd married her mother. "And?"

"Oh, I just let him know what he'd be in for if they dragged me back there. He didn't really want me back anyway. We didn't hit it off and he's more interested in his own little brat now. He said he'd sort Mum out and we wouldn't hear any more about it."

"Dena, it's not that simple."

"Oh, yes, it is," she said confidently. "Mum does what he tells her. Besides, I phoned Social Services too and got hold of the social worker handling my case. Asked her if she knew what happened last time. D'you know, she hadn't even looked it up? Anyway, I told her a few things about Ted."

"What like?"

"How he gave me the creeps when he touched me … that sort of thing. She was all ears."

Millson frowned. "Dena, has Ted ever molested you?"

"No-o. I didn't like it, though, when he put his arms round me and tried to cuddle me."

"But did you let the social worker *think* he molested you?"

"I don't know what she thought," she said evasively. "I didn't say anything that wasn't true. I just gave it a bit of a spin, that's all." She saw the disapproval on his face. "Dad, don't look at me like that. I bet you've had to bend things a bit sometimes."

He laughed and ruffled her hair. "Maybe. But don't tell anyone," he said.

Twenty

Edward Forman's funeral took place two days later in the village of Kirby-le-Soken, where he'd been born. Christine had refused to have him buried in Coggeshall next to his first wife. Millson and Scobie had arrived before the mourners and were seated at the rear of the church with Sandra between them. They were screened from the entrance by a pillar and could watch the people entering without being seen.

Sandra was dressed in black. It was so that Al would take her for one of the family, she explained to Millson, and not give her a second glance. Millson thought the stand-up collar framing her golden curls, and her big blue eyes and baby face, would attract second glances and more from every man who saw her. Certainly, Alan Stigall could hardly fail to notice her, and that was all to the good as far as Millson was concerned. He expected him to turn and run as soon as he saw her, and had taken the precaution of having two of his men discreetly placed near the entrance.

Opposite the church, in the car park of the Red Lion, a man sat waiting in a car. Earlier, he'd been surprised to see

Millson and Scobie drive up and park by the church gates. They had remained in the car, and he'd wondered why they were there. He'd read in the papers the police had identified the skeleton as Barry's, but he wasn't worried. Nor was he worried by the headline, HUNT FOR ALAN STIGALL, on the local newsagents' placards. He hadn't used the name since he left Yeldham over twenty years ago. Changing his name had been easy. He'd simply taken the identity of a boy he knew was emigrating to Australia with his family. He'd sent for a copy of the boy's birth certificate from the Registry of Births and Deaths, used his National Insurance number, and everything had been easy after that. And now there was no one left who knew what he looked like. Except Sandra, of course, and she wouldn't talk.

While he was debating whether to drive away or enter the church and take a seat, another car arrived. A slim woman in a black outfit stepped out, and the two policeman got out of their car and greeted her. He watched the three of them walk towards the church and then the woman turned her head and he saw her full face. He went rigid. He'd know that baby face and those blonde curls anywhere. *It was Sandra!*

The man sank low in his seat, working out the implications. The police had been lying when they told reporters they hadn't found Sandra yet. It was obvious they thought he might show up at the funeral, and had brought her along to eyeball him. She must have opened her big wide mouth and told them about Barry. He clenched his teeth in fury.

The service was due to begin at eleven fifteen and by ten past most of the mourners had arrived and taken their seats. The Forman family, with the exception of Fenella Forman, sat in the front row. Fenella came in later and sat down several rows behind them. Millson looked along the rows for Greg Henderson but saw no sign of him.

Sandra Mitchell had covertly scrutinised each man as he arrived and shown no reaction to any of them. When the vicar took his place in the pulpit, Millson had to accept that Stigall was not going to turn up.

In the car park opposite, the man in the car had decided what to do. Sandra had arrived on her own and would therefore probably leave on her own. He'd follow her and find out where she lived. Then he'd plan the best way to silence her. Not the same way as Sean – that hadn't worked out the way he intended. His plan had been to drown Sean, then drag his naked body to the quicksands by Sandbeach Outfall, which only uncovered at low tide. There his body would have sunk deep down into the soft mud and been lost to sight for ever. But while he was stripping the clothes off him he'd broken free and jumped overboard, then ploughed his way up the mudflats and become trapped in the sludge of Marshhouse Outfall.

The church service ended and the congregation began to follow the coffin along the aisle and out into the autumn sunshine. Millson stepped out of the row to join the end of the cortège and found himself alongside Fenella Forman. She glanced at him, then at Scobie and Sandra Mitchell.

"I'm surprised to see you here, Chief Inspector."

"And I you," he said. "No Mr Henderson?"

"He said he'd come if he could. I assume he couldn't manage it." The luminous eyes gazed up at him. "Why are you here?"

"Duty," he said.

Her eyes moved to Sandra, took in her blonde curls and

pert face. "Really?" she murmured and moved on.

Emerging into the sunshine, Millson and Scobie separated from the mourners and escorted Sandra towards the gate. "Thank you for coming, Sandra," Millson said. "I'm sorry you had a wasted journey."

She shrugged. "So am I."

"I'll whistle up your car." Scobie took out his mobile.

"It's OK. A friend's giving me a lift."

"All the way to London?"

"No, Walton on the Naze. She's lent me her caravan for the weekend … so's I can have a break." Sandra looked across the churchyard to the road. "I can see her waiting. Byesy-bye." She stalked away.

Scobie watched her step into a car and looked at the woman with orange hair sitting at the wheel. "An old Tom," he told Millson.

"Expert, are you, Norris?"

"I did a year in West End Central when I was with the Met," Scobie said. "You learn to spot 'em a mile off." He moved towards the gate.

"Hang on," Millson said. "I'd like a word with Helen before we leave." He sat down on one of the benches.

At the graveside, the committal ceremony ended and the mourners began paying their last respects. Ruth Page saw Fenella turn and walk away.

"Just a moment, Fenella," she called, hurrying after her. "Do you mind returning Bobby's house keys, please?"

"I already have," Fenella said coldly. "To Christine."

"Are you sure?"

"Of course I'm sure. Ask her if you don't believe me."

Ruth said awkwardly, "I have. She says she doesn't have them."

"Oh, does she? Well, we'll soon settle this." Fenella grasped Ruth's arm and propelled her to where Christine Forman was speaking to the vicar.

At the other end of the churchyard Millson came to his feet as Helen Forman approached.

"What have you done with your glamorous companion, Chief Inspector?" She made a brave attempt at a smile.

"She's a witness who can identify Alan Stigall – the man we believe killed Barry Naylor. We thought he might be here."

"Oh, I see. Yes, I read about him in the paper." Some of the sadness went from her face, and she smiled fleetingly as Scobie moved discreetly away. "I presume my aunt and uncle are totally in the clear at last."

"They certainly are." With Scobie out of earshot, Millson was tempted to ask outright if her father had asked her to put an end to his suffering if he became too bad. Then, over her shoulder, he saw Ruth and Fenella coming towards them.

"You asked if anyone else had keys to our house, Chief Inspector," Ruth said. "Well, I don't know if it matters but Fenella gave Bobby's to Steve Gumbrell to hand to Christine the day before Dad died, and he didn't give them to her."

Gumbrell. The connections flashed through Millson's mind. Eddie believing a man at his son's funeral was Alan Stigall ... telling Christine he'd seen him again the day Gumbrell called. *Gumbrell was Alan Stigall.* He rounded on Fenella. "Where's Gumbrell now?"

"He was supposed to be at the funeral. I saw his car in the car park opposite, but it's not there now. You must have frightened him away."

"What make of car?"

"A red Renault. Why? Is he ... ?" But Millson was sprinting for his car, followed by Scobie.

"He must have a good five minutes' start on us," Millson panted, dropping into the driving seat and snapping on his belt. "Whereabouts is this damned caravan site in Walton?"

"There are two. One as you go down the hill into the town, and another on the road up to the Naze."

"Right. Call out the cavalry."

Scobie picked up the handset. After an exchange of messages he said, "We're on our own. The nearest cars are bogged down at Brightlingsea on some Animal Rights demo. Half the division's there. They'll give us back-up as soon as they can."

Millson swore. A moment later he swore again as he rounded a bend and braked sharply to avoid a collision. A farm trailer, the load of hay spilled around it, was lying on its side and blocking the road completely. In the ditch alongside, a dazed farm worker was clambering from a tractor.

"We'll have to double back and go through Kirby Cross," Scobie said.

Millson reversed, slewed the car round and headed back.

On the road to Walton, Gumbrell overtook a lorry, carefully maintaining a position two cars behind the one Sandra was in. He was relieved she seemed to be heading for somewhere local. It would be easier to deal with her here. He decided the best way to make her disappear would be to take her out to sea, wrap her round with anchor chain like a mummy and drop her overboard in Barrow Deep. That way she'd never be found and he'd be safe again. There was nothing to connect him with Eddie Forman.

He hadn't worried when Eddie recognised him six years back when he was at the Yeldham house checking the patio. He hadn't known he was Robert Forman's father, though, and it had been a shock running into him at his funeral. "I know you, don't I?" Eddie had quavered. It was obvious he was senile, so he'd brushed him aside and nobody had taken any notice. But then he'd run into him again, when he was delivering boxes to the house in Coggeshall. Christine Forman had asked him to put them in the garage, and after he'd done so he rang the front door bell to hand her the keys and deliver Fenella's message. "Give her these," Fenella had said. "And tell her from me, Bobby won't be calling any more." But who should open the door to him but the old git himself.

"It's you again! I know you," he'd wailed, his eyes darting all over the place. "I'm going to tell Chrissy."

"You've never seen me before," Gumbrell said. "You're imagining things."

Maybe the old fool was like this all the time now, and no one paid attention to what he said. Or maybe he sometimes spoke sense. He couldn't take the risk. He pocketed the keys, and decided the old man had to be put away quickly before someone took notice of his blathering.

That night he returned and hid in the front garden, watching the house. He saw Christine put Eddie to bed in a front bedroom on his own. So there'd be no one to interfere while he dealt with Eddie. He was old and frail and strangling him would be easy, but that would start a murder hunt. Putting a pillow over his face and suffocating him was better, and they'd think he died naturally in his sleep.

Soon after midnight, the house was in darkness. He

waited another hour and then quietly entered the house using Bobby's keys and crept upstairs. Eddie was heavily asleep. Looking down at him, Gumbrell was reminded of a TV drama he'd once watched. A nurse in an old people's home had despatched patients to the next world when she thought they were suffering too much. She'd poured water down their throats while they were asleep and held their noses so that it went straight into the lungs. The heart stopped almost immediately and they were recorded as having died of heart failure, a common cause of death in old people.

And there was old Eddie, lying on his back, mouth wide open, and next to him on the bedside table, a jug of water and a glass. So that's what he'd done, and it had worked a treat.

He'd decided not to go to the funeral at first. But the Boss Lady had asked him to keep her company and he thought it would look odd if he refused, seeing that he'd gone to the son's. Good thing he had – otherwise he wouldn't have found out what Sandra was up to.

At the caravan site near the Naze, Sandra's friend finished showing her how everything in the caravan worked, and said goodbye. From his car parked on the seafront near the site entrance, Gumbrell watched her leave. He got out of his car and walked into the site. Plenty of time to make his cow of a half-sister sorry for what she'd done.

He looked in the other vans as he approached Sandra's. They were unoccupied. No one within sight or hearing. Perfect. He padded quietly to Sandra's caravan and wrenched open the door.

She whirled round from the sink where she was filling a

kettle, and let out a scream.

"No use you squawking, Sis. There's no one to hear. An' if you squawk again I'll wring your bleeding neck like a chicken's."

"Listen, Al, I—"

"Shut it!" he snarled. Closing the door he moved towards her.

"Slow down," Scobie told Millson as they sped down the hill into Walton. "I think the Martello tower site is closed now. If not, we'll see his car out front in the park. You can't drive into the site itself."

Millson drove slowly past the entrance. The car park was empty. "OK. On down the High Street and along the front," Scobie said.

Driving along the deserted seafront Millson gave a grunt. "There's a red Renault parked ahead."

Scobie nodded. "The site entrance is just beyond it. Let's hope we can find which van she's in."

"And let's hope we're in time," Millson said grimly.

"You shouldn't have done this to me, Sandra." Gumbrell took out the roll of parcel tape he'd brought from his car. "First you put Sean on to me, and he thought he was going to bleed me dry. And now you've been yakking to the police. I'm going to close your cakehole permanently."

"You won't get away with it." She edged away from him and sat down on the sofa-bed. "They'll know it was you."

He smirked. "They'll be looking for Alan Stigall, you dumb bitch, and they're not gonna to find your body."

He eyed her speculatively. Should he kill her now, or wait till they were out on the water? His eyes moved to her legs, encased in sheer black tights … hovered there … returned to her face.

She recognised the look – the look on every punter's face when he was sizing her up. She leaned back on the bed and crossed her legs carelessly, making her skirt ride up.

He leered at her. "You was always good at turning me on, Sis."

This was her only hope, she told herself. Lead him on. Coax him over onto his back, and while he was sighing and moaning grab a kitchen knife from the rack and stick it in him.

He moved forward and sat down beside her. She smiled at him, offering no resistance as he put his hand under her skirt.

Twenty-One

Outside the caravan, Millson crouched by the centre door and motioned Scobie to take the end door. Then together they yanked open the doors, and stepped inside.

Gumbrell scrambled off the divan, dragging Sandra up with him. Snatching a knife from the rack, he pinioned her against him and held the knife to her neck.

"Back off, copper, or I'll cut her throat," he growled.

Scobie, who'd entered the compartment behind under cover of Millson's diversion, held his breath.

"This won't help you, Gumbrell," Millson said sternly. "Put the knife down."

"No way!" Gumbrell pressed the point against Sandra's neck, pricking the flesh. "It's her fault Barry's dead. Has she told you how she used to lead me on?" He jerked her against him. "Go on, Sis, tell him what you were like ... how much you wanted it."

"You bastard!" She stamped her heel viciously on his instep. He gasped with pain and she broke free, turned, and kneed him in the crotch. He doubled forward.

From behind, Scobie leapt through the communicating

209

door and seized his arm, yanking it down against his thigh. The knife clattered to the floor. Before Gumbrell could recover, Millson had his head under his arm in a headlock, and Scobie was pulling his arms back and handcuffing him.

As Millson rattled off the caution, Gumbrell snarled at Sandra, "You're going down with me, slag." He turned his head to Millson. "She only come squawking to you to put herself in the clear. She was the one wanted Barry's mouth stopped, and she helped me bury him."

"He's lying!" Sandra shouted. "It's all lies!"

"Quiet! Both of you," Millson commanded. Outside, a police car roared into the site, siren blaring. "You're safe now, Sandra."

"Yeah, but for how long? S'pose he gets bail."

"He won't," Millson said firmly. "Relax and enjoy your break."

"Yeah, right."

Driving away, Millson said gloomily, "He won't be inside for long, though."

"You reckon not?"

"He was a boy of fifteen who bashed another kid on the head twenty years ago and buried him. That's all the jury will hear, and they'll probably recommend leniency."

"D'you think she was in it with him like he says?"

Millson shrugged. "I don't know. But true or not, it'll weaken the case against him even further."

"What about Eddie's death?"

"Oh, I'm pretty certain Gumbrell killed him, but we'd never prove it. I doubt we could even prove it was murder."

Walking along the corridor to their offices later a WPC intercepted them and handed Scobie a sheet of paper. "Just come in from HQ, Sarge. They've downloaded an e-mail from Gordon Delayney and faxed it on to us."

Scobie scanned the sheet. "Delayney was in Portugal the week Sean Kebble drowned. He left his boat at the Essex Yacht Marina on the Crouch the week before, and asked Bobby Forman to have her brought back to his mooring at Walton." He looked up at Millson. "Perhaps Bobby asked Gumbrell to collect the boat, and Gumbrell used her to dump Kebble on Dengie on his way to back to Walton."

"Except Aubrey Smith told us Gumbrell was out fishing with him that night," Millson said. "Go and see him, Norris. Shake the truth out of him. We'll put off interviewing Gumbrell until tomorrow."

Aubrey Smith looked nervous when Scobie drove into the boatyard. "Boss Lady's at a funeral," he said. "So's Steve."

"No, he isn't, and he won't be coming back," Scobie told him. "It's you I've come to see."

"What's happened to Steve, then?"

"We've arrested him for murder."

"Oh, Gawd! Was it him put that body on Dengie, then?"

"That's right. And you don't want to find yourself charged as an accessory to murder, do you?"

"Oh no … no, I don't," Aubrey's false teeth wobbled as his head shook emphatically.

"You remember telling us Steve was out fishing with you when—"

"Oh, that weren't true! That were a porky! Steve made me say that. I didn't know he'd done a murder, though." Aubrey's eyes blinked rapidly in fear. "I think he did for the guv'nor too."

Scobie's mouth opened in surprise. "What makes you think that?"

"I heard the guv'nor asking Steve about bringing Mr Delayney's *Seaspray* up from the Crouch. Steve told him it had nothing to do with the body on Dengie. But the guv'nor said you was coming to ask more questions in the morning and he'd have to tell you. Then that night the guv'nor had his accident on the *Lady M.*"

"You've got that look on your face that says you know something I don't," Millson said, as Scobie came into his room. "What is it?"

"Aubrey Smith admits his alibi was a complete lie."

Millson's face lit up. "Good. And?"

"He thinks Gumbrell rigged Bobby Forman's accident."

Millson's eyebrows shot up. "Well, there's a turn up for the book." He blew out his cheeks. "Does he have any evidence?"

"Not really." Scobie recounted Aubrey's statement.

Millson frowned. "That's not much good. Besides, Gumbrell has a cast-iron alibi – you checked it yourself. He was in the yacht club bar at the time the accident happened."

When Millson arrived home his daughter asked hopefully, "Will you be going out this evening, Dad?"

"No. Why?"

"I've asked Jackie round to hear my new disc. It's terrific," Dena said. "Thing is, you really need to play it through the speakers to get the full feeling."

He knew what that meant. Maximum volume … pounding sound … walls vibrating. "In that case, young lady, I probably will be going out." He decided to give Helen a call.

Dena was in the kitchen preparing snacks for Jackie and herself when Millson answered the door. Jackie Delayney was wearing satin trousers and a tank top that left her midriff bare. Her navel was hidden by a glittering ornament nestling in it.

"This man Gumbrell you've arrested!," she said excitedly, brushing past him. "I—"

"How d'you know he's been arrested?" Millson demanded.

She said impatiently, "I've just heard it on local radio in my sister's car. I *saw* him the night the *Lady Madonna* blew up."

She and her partner had left the yacht club disco for a while and wandered down to the pontoon moorings, she told him. He gathered they were lying prone on the floor of the club rescue boat when Gumbrell sped up to the pontoons in an inflatable, minutes before the explosion. He'd jumped out and hurried towards the club building.

"He was running," Jackie said.

Millson's eyes lit up. "Are you're sure it was him?"

"Oh yes, I know him well. I've seen him at the boatyard with my father and I've seen him in the club. The point is, he didn't come along the Twizzle from Horsey Mere, he came up Walton Channel."

"I see. And this … um … Walton Channel—"

"Don't you *know*?" She looked at him pityingly. "It leads up from Hamford Water – where the *Lady Madonna* was moored."

So Gumbrell hadn't driven to the yacht club in his car, as he said. Millson's face broke in a smile. He could charge

213

him with Robert Forman's murder as well now. "Jackie, you're wonderful – quite wonderful." He seized her shoulders, pulled her to him, and planted a kiss on her forehead. Still smiling, he went upstairs to change.

"I think your Dad fancies me," Jackie said, joining Dena in the kitchen. "He's just given me a plonker of a kiss."

"Where?" Dena demanded.

"I'm not telling."

"That means it was on your forehead," Dena said. "He kisses me there every night."

"Yes, but you're his daughter. This was different. And he took me in his arms," Jackie said. "I'm going to dream about it tonight."

"You leave my dad out of your dreams, Jacqueline Delayney, or I'll bop you one," Dena said fiercely.

They were on hands and knees positioning the speakers when Millson came downstairs again. "I'll see you two later, then," he said. "Enjoy your music."

As the front door closed, Jackie said, "He's off down the pub, I suppose."

"Oh no," Dena said confidently. "He's put on his best suit and he pongs of aftershave. He's meeting a woman."